THAT WAS SOMETHING

The Art of American Screen Acting: 1912-1960

Vanessa: The Life of Vanessa Redgrave

Barbara Stanwyck: The Miracle Woman

THAT WAS SOMETHING
a novel

DAN CALLAHAN

SQUARES & REBELS
Minneapolis, Minnesota

DISCLAIMER

This is a work of fiction. Names, characters, businesses, places, events, and incidents are either the products of the author's imagination or used in a fictitious manner.

COPYRIGHT

Squares & Rebels
PO Box 3941
Minneapolis, MN 55403-0941

E-mail: squaresandrebels@gmail.com
Online: squaresandrebels.com

Printed in the United States of America.
ISBN: 978-1-941960-10-3
Library of Congress Control Number: 2018907653

A Squares & Rebels First Edition

FOR

Jessica Lange

I

I was looking for the keys to the kingdom, and I found them or thought I did in Manhattan screening rooms, in the half-light and the welcoming dark. There have been times when I have stared up at the movie screen and looked at the people in evening dress walking down a rain-swept promenade at dawn and thought, "What have I done to deserve such pleasure?" A titled lady once came out on a veranda on a sweltering day, sat down, and sipped an ice. "Oh," she purred. "If only this were a sin!"

I found the keys to the kingdom at the Anthology Film Archives when they ran a full retrospective of the films of Michelangelo Antonioni. Some of the prints were so ratty, so frayed, so dirty and jumpy and volatile that you could barely make out the swank Italian players, but the sense was there, all the same. I saw all of them that summer of 1998. All the Antonioni's.

One pivotal night at the Anthology Film Archives, I was trying to see Michelangelo Antonioni's first feature film, *The Story of a Love Affair*, or *Cronaca di un amore*, which sounds prettier, and it truly was the worst print in a series of calamitous prints. I love the Anthology Film Archives, but they have very little money. The seats there were perversely uncomfortable. Sitting in them sometimes felt like sleeping on a board of tiny nails for penance. There was something purgatorial about the large upstairs theater, but it was an affable sort of purgatory, calm, chummy, even.

"I look forward to my demise," announced a small old lady with merry, shining eyes, right before the lights went down in the theater. "Then I will speak to all the great souls of history." She was speaking to a boy who might have been paid to be her companion, but he seemed genuinely fond of her. Whenever there was a kiss in the movie, or even a threat of lovemaking, the old lady who looked forward to her demise would delightedly pucker up her lips and make kissing noises at the screen. It was cute, but I've always felt that kisses should be as silent as possible. When you're kissing parts of someone's body in particular, there's nothing less sexy than the innocuous smacking sound of a kiss.

Antonioni's *Cronaca di un amore* was being projected at the Anthology Film Archives in the summer of 1998. So different. For me, of course, because I was younger, but for everybody too, I think, in Manhattan. That was the first time I heard about Monika Lilac. I might have seen her before, because she was always at screenings as a kind of vaporous, peek-a-boo presence. But that was the first time I heard her name. Ben Morrissey told me about her.

Ben Morrissey was my friend from college. He had only just begun to market himself as a photographer then. He took lots of photos of his friends naked, and this went over well uptown at the Whitney, in a This Is Our Youth kind of way. All the art people with money liked seeing us naked. They liked seeing a fresh new crop of faces, bodies … and minds? They wondered what our particular sensibility would be like.

Ben was sitting next to me. I had dragged him to L'Avventura, and he hadn't liked that movie. He had said something along the lines of the emperor isn't wearing any clothes. But to his credit, Ben felt that he had maybe missed out on something, and so he shyly asked me if he could come see Antonioni's debut with me. I said yes, of course.

Ben has unusually wide shoulders. That's the first thing you notice about him. His waist is surprisingly small in relation to these coat-hanger-like shoulders and this creates a masculine/feminine effect that I find extremely sexy. He has coal dark, slightly curly hair. His voice is so low that it almost sounds like a put-on, it almost sounds goofy. I love Ben, for lack of a better word. I loved seeing him and hearing him and watching him move through space. I loved the furtive, self-deprecating way he talked to women he was attracted to. And I always loved the openly flirtatious "why not?" way he related to me. Ben is very heterosexual, but he liked talking about guys' bodies with me, and I loved talking about women's bodies with him. Ben Morrissey.

I had snuck away from the Midwest and I was sitting in the common room of my New York University dorm, reading War and Peace (I swear!). It was late at night and the common room was deserted. I remember the soothing quality of the low light, the hum of some generator or other making the silence more than silent, if you know what I mean. I was reading about Princess Mary, who was and still probably is my favorite character in that novel, when the elevator doors opened and Ben shuffled out.

He was wearing nothing but gray sweatpants and flip-flops and his luscious sooty curly hair was wet from the shower. I noticed the blond wood shelf shoulders and the wasp waist right away, out of the corner of my eye, and I even got a glimpse of the thick curlicues of hair in the middle of his chest and the slick lethal line of hair leading down to his stomach, which had just a hint of ab definition. Not from working out. Ben never worked out. He just had semi-abs, like someone had drawn them on his stomach, or indicated where they would be. I looked at him just a few seconds too long, so that he definitely noticed me noticing him (he told me that later).

I turned back to my book and pretended to read but couldn't make head nor tail of whatever poor repressed Princess Mary was doing or feeling. Ben had sauntered over to the pop machine and was just standing there looking at his options. The light was hitting his body in just the right way so that I could make out two dimples in the small of his back. And then, I swear, he put his hands on his hips and *bent over* slightly, just slightly.

When I asked him about this later, Ben's sleepy black stoner eyes flitted around with a hectic remembrance. "Yeah, yeah, I was fucking with you. You know, you were this lonely little gay boy and you were reading that great big book all by yourself in the common room ... I mean, who actually sat in that common room but you?! I knew you needed a little fun or whatever. And my body was kind of nice, and I knew you saw that and liked that, whatever. You looked at me and then you got all flushed and nervous and started reading your book again, and, you know, I found that pretty charming, that's all."

And he made something of a routine of it. Or at least that's what I felt at the time. I think I had some classes with him, but Lord, who can remember classes at this point, not me. It's a wonder I ever finished *War and Peace*. Ben would cop to that first time, but he refused to see his continuing "why not?" soda pop machine seduction of me in the common room as anything more than a comic routine. He vehemently denied it at first, but then he got into it as a story and would even do it as a story and act it out for the girls he was seeing.

Of course these girls found the story attractive (Ben didn't ever date girls who wouldn't have found that story attractive), so it worked out just fine for him. It's not like the story made him look gay or something. It just made him look open and fun, and those qualities are sexy. And sexy is what Ben Morrissey is and probably always will be. Just say his name in front of certain girls and a few guys and watch how flustered and excited and high-strung they get. And he's not even in the room. You're just saying his name, and that's enough.

There came a point when Ben asked me out. To dinner and a movie. Some straight boys in Manhattan by the late '90s felt like they could ask gay boys on quasi-dates without it being weird. Something had preceded his asking me, something physical. It was Valentine's Day, I swear (that I have to remember), and we were waiting around for a teacher to come to class, probably. Ben and I were talking. We were never introduced or anything, but in this school milieu we just slowly fell into talking with each other sometimes for a few moments.

Ben is so friendly that he talks to everybody, and he really does try to like everybody or find something to like about them. The thing about Ben Morrissey is, if he likes you, you feel like you probably are likable. And he never goes too far. Lots of people are so insecure and unhappy with themselves, and Ben always knows just how much attention to give to someone without getting into trouble. He's not one of these charismatic people you hear about who turn their entire attention to you and make you feel amazing and then leave you totally in the lurch when they turn their attention to someone else. Ben gives a little specific attention to everybody, within reason. Ben Morrissey just makes life so much better and so much more endurable, let's face it. I still feel that.

So it was Valentine's Day, and we were sitting waiting in one of those ill-lit classrooms that make you want to just curl up and go to sleep and never wake up, and Ben was fucking with me in his exploratory way. "Do you have a date or a sweetheart or whatever?" he asked me. Twinkly little stud eyes, a smile that takes over his whole face and makes you smile back at it. I said no, no I didn't.

"Why is that?" he asked. OK, Ben can be kind of jerky sometimes, but I swear, he does it with such style, such finesse. Don't think I'm unreliable. I'd love it if I could make you feel almost exactly what it's like when Ben Morrissey is focusing on you and smiling at you and asking about you. He's so smart in this warm way, and he makes you feel that he sees everything about you that isn't all that great and he doesn't mind. Everything about him is, "Don't worry, I like you."

So, yeah, "Why is that?" he asked, and I fumbled around. He let out this little laugh and patted me on my left shoulder. Yes, I still remember which shoulder, of course. "It's OK, man, you don't have to explain yourself to me," he said. Ben is the kind of guy who says, "Man," and he'll even do "dude" sometimes, but not too often. I should explain further that at this time, straight guys seemed to feel secure enough to toy with gay boys and thought that it would make them seem cool with their girls and just cool in general, but a lot of gay boys were still closeted in college, in Manhattan, in the late '90s. I was still closeted. And that was miserable, but so what. In all honesty, I'm almost glad I was closeted then just so that Ben could see me as a kind of project, somebody to help out in his Ben Morrissey way.

I can't remember how it happened, but it must have been somewhat abrupt, what happened next. Because I can't imagine what pretext Ben would have had to do what he did with me in front of everyone. I can't

DAN CALLAHAN

imagine what the transition would be. Ben put his large weight-of-the-world straight-boy hand on my right shoulder this time and gracefully led me up out of my seat and before I knew it he had put my right hand on his waist (that waist!) and pulled my left hand up and stared straight into my eyes and started to dance with me around the room.

Maybe I had been telling him that my grandmother used to teach dancing and that she had taught me some steps? I'm six feet tall and Ben is six feet, two inches, so I was looking up at him. We were really awkward at first, because I was completely panicked (I was almost hyperventilating) and I had no idea what was going on. It was like a dream but it was happening. It went badly at the start, but Ben just looked at me and laughed a little. Don't worry, I like you. He asked if I knew any dances, and I said I knew the fox trot and all these other things and he laughed again and said that we should just keep it simple.

I remember that everybody in the room was staring at us but trying not to stare, you know? I particularly remember how the girls reacted. Some of them had had their own encounters with Ben, some of them wanted to, all of them were interested in him in some way. And when they saw Ben trying to dance with me, they looked at each other and talked softly in each other's ears and smiled shyly, and I could feel that they really liked what he was doing, or trying. I think that it somehow gave them hope for themselves, but I also think that it made them feel that Ben was never going to just be with them. Ben was going to be with everybody at once, just for long enough. There was no point in getting possessive about him. He was just there to be enjoyed.

I think probably a few of them were contemptuous of that. There would be some girls at parties who would try to make fun of Ben, turn him into some kind of joke, but it never worked, and even the least self-aware of them knew that it never worked. He wasn't going to be your boyfriend or your husband, and you couldn't fit him into a stereotype of a player or ladies' man or whatever (*or whatever*, that's pure qualifying Ben Morrissey talk) and you couldn't make him a joke.

Let's stick to something simple, he said, and so I said that we could do the box waltz. You just make a box with your feet, it's simple, that's what I said. Ben said he had never done that before, but he would try it. And so I started doing the box waltz with him, and suddenly it wasn't awkward at all. Most people can do the box waltz in one place just fine, one box, as it were, but Ben right away started dancing me around the room and the boxes we made with our feet were almost ridiculously perfect. Our bodies moved together perfectly.

We were spinning around the room, and I remember that Ben was very decisive about making the movements *land* as movements. We're here, and now we're here, and now we're here. And he was laughing a little and I was even smiling because it was so perfect, this dance. It was like jumping off a roof and not falling to the ground to go splat but hitting a point of suspension in the air and not quite flying maybe but floating, not falling, maybe touching the tip of your toes on the various cars parked along the street. With everybody watching!

Our dance stopped at some point, of course. It couldn't have lasted long. When it clicked, it was just perfect, perfect, perfect and then sit down and laugh. And I guess a class eventually began, but who cares, no one remembers that. So many straight guys, if they had danced with me like that (on Valentine's Day!) would have made it a joke afterward to save face. But Ben very clearly didn't want that. He felt that what had happened was special (he told me later). And so he even talked about it, a little wonderingly, and very respectfully. And he must have enjoyed the tickled, skeptical looks on the girls' faces as he mentioned me and our dance. It gave them pleasure, complicated pleasure, pleasure that was like a large house with all kinds of rooms to look through, run through, tiptoe through, fall asleep in.

So one day after class, in front of New York University's Tisch Building on Broadway, Ben asked me if I wanted to get dinner and see a movie sometime. I said yeah, um, that would be great. He smiled that smile and he walked down Broadway ahead of me, pulling one girl into his embrace and then another further on ahead. He's very touchy-feely in a way that I think of as Californian, for some reason. Ben spent his summers in northern California with his father when he was a kid. He has a way of touching people on their necks or shoulders that never seems intrusive. He makes it seem natural, slightly sexy but not particularly sexual.

We met for dinner at a restaurant on 7th Street and Fifth Avenue that had two levels. Light red upholstered booths. New American cuisine, whatever that is. I think Ben might even have said that, whatever that is. I don't remember exactly what we talked about, but I do remember that we were on the second floor of the restaurant and that Ben created this atmosphere that made me feel we were doing something excitingly furtive, something unusual, something against the grain. We saw a movie on Third Avenue and 12th Street. I remember what the movie was, but this movie was so trivial that I don't need to tell you about it. But I do need to tell you about what happened when I went back to the dorm with Ben. Rubin Hall, on Fifth Avenue and 10th Street.

We drank some cheap red wine from a jug in Ben's room, and of course he got out his camera. Ben nearly always had a camera around his neck. He never used it aggressively but caressingly, as if the camera were an extension of his long-fingered, expressive hands, with their creamy white wrinkled skin. His fingers looked like satin leg warmers clinging to a blonde girl's calf. I told him about my unhappiness and loneliness and the loneliness of my past and all that, and he nodded a lot, as if he knew this was to be expected. Gradually my use of "they" became "he," and I'm pretty sure that Ben gently led me to "he." I got a little squirmy at one point, and so Ben said decisively, "OK, you're a gay guy, that's fine. I knew that when I danced with you. And you cross your legs at the knee! So whatever, it's fine, man."

When I got to a particularly bad experience, though, something that I had never told anybody before, Ben's face changed and the slight smile he usually wore was put away. He stood up, all six feet two inches of him, and he said, "Stand up, man," and I did, and he put his arms around me and hugged me, not for a couple of seconds or thirty seconds or whatever, which might have been more expected. I would guess that Ben hugged me in his motionless, solid way for four to five minutes, and when he let go of me, I was changed. I really was. I knew that I would never be unhappy in the way I had been before again. Because I knew that I would always be able to remember those four or five minutes.

We got drunk and drunker, and I wasn't an experienced drinker yet. It's so wonderful when you start drinking heavily and you're not an experienced drinker and you're with somebody like Ben who you want to talk to and listen to. After The Big Hug (which is what I called it later in letters to Ben), we got very silly drunk and playful, and Ben did a lot of teasing and tickling and so forth. He showed me some photos he'd been taking of girls he'd been seeing. I probably would have been impressed by anything he showed me, but I think even then I realized that Ben was a first-class photographer.

It's hard to define photographic talent, but I know now that Ben had really studied the major photographers and was learning everything he could from them. He talked a lot about Richard Avedon that night, and he showed me some Avedon photos, and I didn't like them at all, but I could see that Ben was using aspects of Avedon's technique to leap off into his own landscape, his own kindly sensual vibe.

A lot of the girls had posed naked for Ben. The flush of the wine neutralized any puritanical Midwestern notions I might have had about their nudity. Ben wasn't exploiting them, and he wasn't just showcasing what was conventionally attractive about them. He was looking for something else. Even if I didn't know Ben personally, even to a totally untrained eye, you can see that he's using the camera to look deeply into a person and capture something about them.

But he's into the purely physical, too, in his off-hours. Ben loves breasts. He can talk about them in great detail for a long time, and I love the way his face just lights up when he does. With time, I got to be a connoisseur of them, too. Ben loved smallish, hard breasts, but he particularly loved a pair of breasts that dipped slightly and then somehow came back up again. There must be a word for that. They go slightly downward and then the nipple somehow points back up. You see a lot of that with girls who have smallish breasts, this dip-down-nipple-back-up thing. The ideal is probably Monica Bellucci. If you haven't noticed, type Bellucci's name into Google and have a look sometime if you need a pick-me-up.

When Ben talked about these girls he had photographed, his voice got kind of reverent and his face looked childlike, innocent, but with a mixture of skin-licky impurity, too. He could be talking about the camera and the lights he was using and being very technical, and he could also go into slightly gooey talk about these girls and how much he loved this and that in them, but when he sensed my attention wandering, he would push a button and say something just absolutely *filthy* about them or something he had done or wanted to do to their bodies, and I would laugh. "Do you want to see some guys?" he asked, finally. "I don't have too many. OK, I only actually have three guys who have posed for me. But I need more! I'm working on that! Maybe you can help me?"

So I looked at the guys. Two of them I knew from school, and they were straight, and they had taken their shirts off, and they looked slightly abashed. They had kept their pants on. Then there was another guy who Ben told me he had been friends with in high school but didn't see much anymore. This guy was naked in the photos, and there were lots and lots of photos of him, and he was skinny and fragile and very feminine-looking. "Guys used to beat him up all the time," Ben said. "He wasn't tough in any way, you know? He was really soft, and he'd always come in with a black eye or something. And this is going to sound weird, but the black eye made him even prettier or something. And the bruises he had. The black eyes and the bruises looked almost like, I don't know, something he put on to look even prettier. Does that sound weird?" I said no, but it did sound weird to me then. Less so now.

We drank some more, and the room started to spin a little bit. The desk lamp and the bed and the kitchen stove and the pizza boxes on the floor started to look like sheets of rain were pouring down them and the furniture was shimmery and silly as we were and there were no problems that couldn't be solved. I don't drink anymore. I had to stop, but I love drinking, or at least I love what it can do when you're nineteen and in a dorm room with someone you like. So the things in the room were shimmery spinning, and Ben was telling me more about this boy who used to get beat up a lot. "I shouldn't tell you this," he said.

"What?" I asked, and giggled. I'm a giggler.

"You're a giggler," he said, and I giggled some more. "OK, OK, I tried to fuck him once," Ben said. "I put it in, and I pumped a few times, but I just wasn't into it, and so I had to stop." I said, "Oh," I think. "And he was really feminine," Ben said. "Everything about him was feminine. Maybe if I'd dressed him up? He said he would do that for me. Put on women's clothes. That might have worked. Will you pose for me, man?"

I said sure, of course. I was so drunk. So was he, so the first photos we took were so disastrous that we laughed about them for a long time afterward. They were mainly out of focus and there's no generous way to describe me as a subject in them. But gradually the furniture in the room stopped shimmering and we sobered up just enough. That's tricky, sobering up just enough to keep a vestige of the initial drunken euphoria, but we managed that night. "Take your shirt off," Ben said, very casually, but just hearing him say those words made me hard, of course. Well, at that age, tying my shoelaces made me hard, let alone Ben Morrissey telling me, commanding me!, to take my shirt off.

"Huh," he said when I had done as I was told. "You're not as scrawny as I thought you were." Click, click, click. I naturally got into different angular positions. "You move really weirdly but really well," he said. Ben's compliments are always very specific. "I think your body would react really well to working out," he said. "You have distinct possibilities." Click, click. "You have distinct possibilities," he said again, in a more distracted tone of voice, very Warren Beatty. I giggled, and he tickled me. "Giggler," he said, and he tickled me and poked at me in a way I imagine a big brother would have. I'm an only child. Lots more clicks, and then Ben said, "OK, now you're going to take your pants off for me, unlike those other two guys who are just total fucking cowards, whatever, right?"

Suddenly I was scared and I felt like this might be a bad idea, that I didn't know this guy really, right? "I don't know," I said.

"You're safe with me, Bobby, OK?" Ben said, in his very low, most serious voice. "You know that, right? We have a thing together, I can feel it already. This isn't just a one-time thing. I have a feeling I'm probably going to want to take photos of you my whole life, OK? With your pants on, and with your pants off. I want to *see* you, OK?"

I looked down at the floor. "I'm a virgin," I said.

"I know that," Ben shot back, really quickly. "We're going to take care of that. Let me take care of that for you. I'll find you a guy. I can find you a guy, I promise. We'll take care of that. Now take your pants off and let me see the rest of your body. You know you want to!" I giggled. "Aren't you pagan enough?" he asked. I took my pants off.

Ben clicked clicked and made fun of my underwear. "No wonder you're still a virgin! Fruit of the Loom is a fucking boner killer, dude! What, did your Mom buy that for you? We're going to get you some underwear. You, my friend, are going to be one *hot fucking gay guy* when we are done with you."

Lots of clicks as I danced around the room and we were very laughy and smiley and I was extremely giggly because I felt that my gigglyness charmed Ben, and I wanted to keep on charming him. "You have the tiniest butt," Ben said. "Like, you have no butt at all! I don't even see one, where is it?" I giggled. "But you know, we can work with that. You're weird. Everything about you that should be a minus is a plus, I think. Like, even the fact that you have no butt at all is *charming*. You fucking giggly nerdy skinny charmer," he said.

"Is this the way you talk to girls?" I asked.

"Um, pretty much," he said, click click. "But you're a guy, so some adjustments need to be made, obviously. I don't have a set routine, I swear. I try to, um ..." click click, "I try to really see the person in front of me, OK? And you know," click click, "Like ... *love* them. Or love something about them. And make them feel loved and sexy." Click, click, click. "Not everybody, make no mistake," he said. "I pick and choose." Click click.

"You pick and choose your victims," I said and giggled.

"Yeah," Ben said, almost in a whisper.

"I like being your victim," I said. Click, click, click, click, click.

"I had a feeling you would," Ben said. "Take your underwear off ... take them down, get them down." I stood there for a couple of seconds. "Do you trust me?" he asked.

"Yes," I said, without even having to think about it.

"Then let me ... let me do this. Let me see you and make you sexy," he said, and he was looming over me and he pulled my underwear down to my ankles and my hard-on hit his head as he got up, and we both laughed. "It is completely OK that you have a boner," Ben said. "I'm a good-looking guy and I know exactly how much I excite you." Ben had a way of saying things like that that was:

A. Completely matter-of-fact.

B. Deeply, deeply silly.

C. So baldly manipulative that while you were laughing you were feeling just how true a statement it was.

"But this isn't porn, so I'm going to need you to turn around for these next shots and show off your completely non-existent butt, which we are somehow going to turn into something extremely sexually desirable to every hot gay guy in Manhattan when I'm a famous photographer," he said.

Now, the funny thing about that is. Lots of guys and girls who are basically dumb but energetic and filled with unwarranted self-esteem at that age will say things like that, about one day being a famous whatever, and even then you just have to roll your eyes inwardly. But when Ben said something like that, at nineteen, it was just a fact, with only the lightest dusting of irony, a little confectioner's sugar to make the undoubted prospect of his future fame go down even easier.

So I did as I was told. The photos came out better than I expected. I looked a little weird, because I am a little weird, and because Ben was shooting me in that way of his, which was already almost fully formed. I looked off-kilter but the honest tenderness with which I was shot made me as sexy as I possibly could be then. He touched me a few times while I was naked and he was shooting me, on the shoulders, on my waist, pushing my legs into even more angular positions. And suddenly he was all business, because he knew he had to be. I was naked and he was taking pictures of me, but he made me feel like we were doing a job together that needed to be done, and only when he was done click clicking did he slip back into his teasing mode with me. Ben put down his camera and said, "Put your clothes back on, sweetie, we're going to drink some more on the roof."

It was maybe 3 AM then. Very dark, the darkest dark. Manhattan was still new to me. We got upstairs with our jug of wine and Ben pulled on the door that would have led us to the roof, but it was locked. "Fuck," I said. I was learning to swear. I come from a place in the Midwest where a movie is considered good if it has "no curse words." So saying, "Fuck" then was a big deal, it's all a big deal. Ben lifted up one of his long, long strong legs and kicked the door. He kicked it again harder. He kicked it a third time, and it opened. He had meant to impress me by kicking in this door, and I was impressed. I still am. My knight in shining armor! My heterosexual dreamboat!

We drank some more on the roof and talked some more. Ben talked a lot about girls. I remember he said, "You need to have sexual ambitions, my friend." He put his hand on my right shoulder, not lightly as he usually did, but heavily, as if to stress the point he was making. "Without sexual ambitions, there isn't too much point. Even if they're outlandish, whatever, you just go for it. Even if you don't make it, you'll have fun if you approach it correctly." I was a pretty woebegone little nineteen-year-old at that point, but I understood exactly what Ben meant, and I understood that it related to him. It meant, take what you can get from me, but don't expect anything. It was getting cold. Ben put his jacket around me. He was a very courtly date in many ways. I'm surprised he didn't buy me a flower or corsage or whatever. Whatever!

So it was starting to get light, and Ben had this idea that we had to walk across the Brooklyn Bridge. Of course, right? Because that's the kind of idea that came to us at 4 AM or so then. So we started walking through the nearly deserted streets, and it was so chilly in cozy Washington Square Park, and we had only a rough idea of where the Brooklyn Bridge was, but we had fun getting lost. At a certain point we got tired for a little bit, so we stretched out on the grass in front of a large glass office building downtown. We were side by side, and I looked over at Ben, who had his eyes closed.

The sun was hitting him in just the right way, and I noticed that he had a little red indentation on his right cheekbone. Was it a scar of some sort? I was pretty uninhibited at that point, so I reached over and ran my fingers over the scar, or the indentation, or whatever it was. Ben was almost asleep, but he smiled slightly at my touch. Somehow it was much more intimate than if I had put my hand in his crotch, you know? That would have been expected, but this was a much deeper touch, a much more vulnerable thing. I had found a flaw in his looks, and he knew it. And he must have also known that this tiny flaw would become for me the most attractive thing about him physically. I had noticed it. I'm sure some girls had. We were the ones who had noticed The Scar on Ben Morrissey's Face. "You're sweet," he whispered.

We got up together and wandered some more around the little streets downtown, off the grid. These were streets where people worked in finance, and they had a very different feeling from the stinky funky old hippie streets of the East and West Village that I was getting to know. They were orderly and dull, like jury duty. Bring a book. We finally found the Brooklyn Bridge, and I swear, the sun was dawning as we walked across it. So romantic, right? Ben looked so tall next to me. It was one of those moments when it felt like I was watching us walk across the Brooklyn Bridge at dawn. I can see it that way now, but I saw us objectively exactly that way at the time, too. Ben was such an expert scene-maker.

"So Bob … Bobby?" Ben said.

"Bobby is good," I said. I'm sure I was blushing.

"So Bobby, let me just say this. I needed more guys for my photos, and I'm sure that in the back of my mind I saw you as a potential conquest, right?" I was wildly flattered that Ben Morrissey could refer to me as "a potential conquest" in any way, and yes, he knew that, he's smart. "And I got what I wanted, I got some good shots, I think, we'll take more, is that OK?"

"That's more than OK," I said. I think this might have been the first, I don't know, *adult* thing I ever said?

"You're just a little weirdo exhibitionist, aren't you?" Ben said, and he poked me and tickled me in that big brother way he had. We were maybe halfway across the bridge at this point. I was staring up at all the cables and I think my mouth was open in a starry, la-di-da smile. I was starting to play a part for Ben, put together a persona for him. I do that with everybody I really love, I put together a whole detailed performance of myself just for them. Depending on whom I'm with, this performance can vary pretty drastically.

"I just don't want you to think later that I was being too shady or something," Ben said. His face was really sincere, and his dark fan-like eyebrows were pushed up into a really cute peak so that I could see he was serious, or trying to be serious. "I'm maybe a little shady, but just a little bit. I really genuinely like you, OK?"

"OK," I said. I could have died of pleasure right then.

"Will you be my friend?" Ben asked. It was totally naked emotionally, this question, a risk, and it gave me the opportunity to have a little power, and I loved that, too.

"Yes," I said. "Yes, yes, yes." And then I said, "There's nothing original about me, except a little original sin." Jane Bowles. Which I told him later, because he thought it was my line, my thought, though it might as well have been.

Ben wanted me to talk about guys and what I liked about them, but I was too shy for that then. "I like looking at guys' asses," Ben said, but it didn't sound particularly sincere. I giggled.

"OK, I wish I could be more into guys," he said, sweetly. "They're so hairy, right? And I don't like that. I like that smooth skin on a young lady." I loved the formal way he said "young lady" at that time. It was classic him, both serious and amusingly non-serious. And then he went into another breast monologue, at something of a fever pitch for him. His voice was almost always laidback, or "laidback," except when he circled back to favorite topics. I think he could tell that I was getting a little bored by his breast talk, impassioned though it was, and so he slung one of his long, long strong arms around me as we walked. We were almost to the end of the bridge then. I think Ben's arm was around my shoulders, hugging me to him, for five minutes or so. I was so happy then that I got teary.

We had breakfast in a diner on the other side in Brooklyn. That was the first time I was ever in Brooklyn. Everybody lives in Brooklyn now (I do, have for years), but in 1996 I thought I would never leave Manhattan. Brooklyn to me was this place you left if you were unlucky enough to have been born there. I had a 1950s idea of Brooklyn. People in the Midwest still do.

When we were done with our runny eggs and buttered slivers of toast, we walked and walked for a long time more in the early morning light and eventually reached a spot where you could look out over to the Statue of Liberty. Ben lifted his endless arm up in the air and posed with an imaginary torch and I giggled. He did look like a statue for a few moments. We were suddenly very tired again, exhausted even. Ben found this little stone alcove thing (there were a row of them) and he climbed into it. It was deep enough so that his crazy-long legs just fit into it. "Come in here with me and rest, sweetie-pie," he said. That was the first "sweetie-pie," I think.

I got into the little stone alcove with Ben, and I felt really self-conscious lying down so close to him. We lay there for a couple of seconds unmoving. We didn't quite fit. We were both breathing heavily. "Here, put your head on my chest so that we can rest easier," he said, and he roughly pulled me over on top of him. I could barely breathe I was so excited, but I concentrated on the rhythm of his breathing, his chest going up and down, and this started to lull me. I was so tired. Before he slipped away into sleep, Ben said quietly, "My friend, you deserve a cuddle after posing for those pictures for me, you're a gutsy guy. Just think of my big sexy body as your pillow, man." I giggled.

"You know you want my dick in you," he sighed.

"Shut up," I said. I didn't actually, I was way too scared (a virgin!), but I *loved* hearing him talk like that and tease me. He's the best tease. He's not a mean tease. He's a tender tease.

II

Ben was doing a project that semester where he was supposed to work with only one model, and he picked me, so I posed for Ben exclusively for five or six months. I would stay over at his dorm room (he had a room to himself for some reason, maybe family connections?), and he would make me breakfast in the morning. Scrambled eggs with chives, with some cold sour cream and tabasco sauce on the side. We would drink black coffee all day until we were bouncing off the walls, and then we would start drinking beer and wine, an intensely pleasurable cycle.

I soon found out that Ben's teacher that semester was a middle-aged gay guy, Mike Whitehead. He was really gross and nudgy and not into me at all but totally into Ben, of course. The gay teachers at NYU ignored the usually forlorn, damaged gay boys and focused all their attention on the hottest winner straight boys, who toyed with them for grades and for narcissistic kicks.

I was walking down University Place with Mike Whitehead and Ben once, and they were having a talk about all the girls Ben was seeing or trying to see. Finally Mike sputtered something good-humored but insulting to Ben about his supposed womanizing. I was walking behind them, nearly unseen or unnoticed. Ben looked back at me and then at Mike and said, "Well, Bobby Quinn has a thing for me." He said it as if my having a thing for him was a large point in his favor. And it was, I guess. Or maybe, in his kind way, Ben just chose to see it like that and made everybody else see it like that, too.

We were shooting some photos in one of the bare rooms with wooden floors set aside for such things at school when Mr. Whitehead came in. We looked up. I was startled but Ben seemed to expect to be interrupted. We were both clothed. "Oh, I thought you boys would be in your underwear by now!" Mike said in his spluttering way. He was always throwing his hands around when he talked and he had the slightly protruding eyes of a compulsive masturbator.

"Get out of here," Ben said in a soft voice that clearly got across who was naturally in charge in this situation. Mike sputtered something and closed the door.

"Do you see the way he looks at me?" Ben asked.

"I don't like him," I said.

"Neither do I," Ben said. "He thinks he's set something up between us. Maybe he has. But he's beside the point, man."

I was either "man" or "sweetie" or, when he really loved me, "sweetie-pie." Right now, I needed to be "man." I kept my clothes on for that session. We did a lot of nudes, but the nudes weren't for the show that would be graded at the end of the semester. "These are just for us," Ben said, "for now, and we'll use them later." It was never "I." It was always "we."

Ben and I were a team, and when I talked to some of his girls, I found that he spoke to them in much the same way, always "we." Some people just have authority, and you're so lucky if you meet them and get swept along by their energy and they also happen to be basically nice. And self-aware. Self-awareness couldn't be more attractive to me. I always try to detail all my flaws to someone I'm getting to know before anybody can possibly be aware of them yet, and I try to make them entertaining. But there's nothing worse, of course, than a self-aware person who tells you what a loser they are and all you can do is agree with them and try to get as far away from them as possible, because self-awareness like that can be contagious.

So the photos were shown, and Mike knew that he had a real contender in Ben, but he couldn't have known just how far Ben would move up the art world ladder and how fast. The Internet hadn't quite happened yet (I didn't even have an email address then), and so Ben put together a portfolio of his best photos, a lot of which, I'm sorry, were of me, and sent them off to every editor and gallery owner and art dealer he knew, and he knew pretty much all of them. Not only did he know their names, he knew their quirks, their soft spots, what they did in bed, where they liked to go for dinner, you name it.

Ben had been raised alone, during most of the year, by his distracted mother, who did something vaguely in the arts or with arts management and seemed to know everybody cultural or vaguely cultural in Manhattan. Ben was ideally situated to get in with the in art crowd, and fast, and he swept me along with it.

After college, Ben was waiting on tables at a place in midtown called Sweet Rosie O'Grady or something, and my very nice parents had very nicely given me a small amount of money as a graduation present, and I was beginning to pick up my first freelance writing jobs. So we still had time to stay up all night and drink and so forth. I had moved into a one-bedroom apartment in Chelsea with a friend who soon left to study abroad and left me the place to myself for a few months.

While we were still at school, Ben had done his best to hook me up with the few out gay guys, but none of them did anything for me. They weren't Ben Morrissey, right? They were so pitifully, so abjectly *not* Ben Morrissey. Some of them were nice and most of them were very feminine, and I was prejudiced against feminine guys then. That's called conditioning. This conditioning meant that I was still a virgin when I was twenty-one and finished with school and living in Chelsea by myself.

Ben was seeing about three girls at once, as usual. We would sometimes hang out with one or even two of them, and mainly they tried to court me because they knew I meant a lot to Ben. I liked this courting, and I responded in kind. You're young, you drink a lot, things get pretty experimental. One time we wound up back at my place, Ben and me and a girl named Tanya, who was Russian and had a thick accent.

Tanya did installations, and she still does. I can't pretend that I like them too much, or understand them. To me it just looks like a lot of detritus on the floor, but I can be lowbrow like that. I might not have liked or understood her work overly much, which has been well enough reviewed through the years, but how could I not be into Tanya herself? There's something about certain Eastern European women that stirs me as deeply as I can be stirred by a woman. A certain brusqueness, a deep, burned impatience.

Tanya was like that stereotype I have, in some ways, but she could be silly, too, very un-Russian, really. I'm most drawn to people who can be truly and deeply silly for extended periods of time. She could be silly without ever losing a basic dignity and apartness, and this created the tension that made her so attractive. To Ben, she was just one of his girls, I think. She was one of my favorites of his girls, but I don't think he would say the same. He always tried not to play favorites with us.

So what did Tanya look like? There was something a touch non-descript about her looks, actually. Her face was round and her eyes were as small as Ben's were. She's gotten thinner with the years. "I liked Tanya better when she was a little fleshier," I said to Ben once. "You would," Ben said. He can be cryptic. She's a make-up girl, she wears a lot of it, and when she does different things with make-up she can look drastically different. Maybe that's why I can't quite describe her looks as I can describe Ben's, or Monika Lilac's. Ben hadn't even seen or heard of Monika Lilac yet, I don't think. She's a sorceress, she makes you forget the first time, it's all just a romantic blur with her. Oh sweetie-pie, summers with Monika.

In any event, Ben and Tanya and I were all smashed and in my Chelsea one-bedroom on 20th Street off Eighth Avenue with the exposed red brick. The red brick was ... exposed! Sexy, right? The red brick is such a slut, it should cover up sometimes. Did Ben say that? He might have. Or I might have said something close to it. Ben and I had the kind of relationship where we were so often together and so often chatting and doing little routines that who said what first starts to fade and doesn't really matter. It was just part of our long-running friendship vaudeville act.

So we were all drunk and all sitting on the futon in the front room against the slutty uncovered red brick, and I was sitting in between them, and Ben and Tanya started kissing each other *over* me, lightly at first but then full-on devouring. Her semi-large breasts were lightly brushing my chest. I was stone still. Just feeling them over me. Sort of moving into her and becoming her a little bit as he kissed her and she kissed him back.

They broke the kissing for a couple seconds, and Ben said to me, "Go into the bedroom and don't shut the door and just listen to us." I did as I was told, because it was exactly the right thing to do. Not watch, not be involved. Just listen. And imagine. Ben wanted to keep my interest in him high, and he knew instinctively that it would stay very high if I heard this purely auditory version of what he was like in bed but didn't see it or feel it.

They were noisy enough. The noises didn't feel too performed, although they must have been. Tanya had heard him order me to the bedroom and keep the door open. She was aware of my presence. Tanya could hold her liquor, she was never unaware. I wonder exactly what she felt about it. Did she like my listening? Was it all the same to her? Did it annoy or offend her? I hope not. I couldn't say. She didn't seem to be performing for me, or for him, but she didn't hold back, either. Actually, thinking back on it now, she probably did hold back some. She made him work for it. He had to work really hard to get a response from her sexually. Ben himself let out these extremely guttural groans. Very him, a little silly, a little serious. Very hot, really. And of course I wanted to see him, I still hadn't seen him naked, just shirtless, and he was a guy who was shirtless a lot, even outside on the street in coldish weather. Because, why not?

I once interviewed Marian Seldes, a lovably and exaggeratedly gracious theater actress of advanced years. She began to detail the many, many difficulties she had experienced in the company of an older star actress, Judith Anderson, when she was young. Then she stopped herself and said, "Well, why not? She was a superb actress." I didn't quite follow her line of reasoning then and I still can't. Anderson was a superb actress, and so that gave her the go-ahead to be strict and overly harsh, why not?

Still, I like Marian's "Why not?" I like "Why not?" but I like "Nevertheless" even more. I think what this great lady of the theater really meant was "Nevertheless, she was a superb actress," but she was more generous and gave Anderson a "Why not?" instead. Ben was being manipulative with me. Why not? Or nevertheless, he was still Ben Morrissey, and he had been blessed, and he blessed me with his presence and with the heartfelt way he toyed with me and kept me in his orbit.

I turned twenty-one, and I was still a virgin, and Ben was getting comically and actually impatient with me. There was a lot of, "Well, I'm just going to have to do the job myself!" and grabbing and tickling, and of course I loved that and wanted to keep it going for as long as possible or even ... well, all right, I semi-secretly and shyly hoped that Ben would actually follow through on his jokey threats, maybe. I was like a gambler at a gaming table waiting to see what everybody else had in their hands. I was scared, but I was also ready.

One night we were drinking even more than usual, and Ben said, "Quinn, you don't want your virginity to be your *trademark*, do you?" His touchy-feely relations with me finally seemed maddening. He brought me to a fever pitch physically and then left me to see a girl. Erica? Amy? One of the many Jennifers? Not Tanya. Tanya was through with him at that point. But they have gone to each other's openings through the years, and her face got awfully surprised as Ben's openings got bigger and bigger.

In any event, I lost my virginity that night, out of sheer impatience and frustration, but only incrementally and not quite technically. I tell people that I walked into Rawhide Bar on 21st Street and Eighth Avenue a boy and I limped out a man, wocka, wocka, wocka, but that's just a joke line. I steered clear of major sexual acts at first.

I never hooked up at this time with boys my own age, mainly because they never seemed to be around at the bars I went to in Chelsea. But also because a few of them rejected me very cruelly and verbally. And so I learned to offer myself up as a kind of virgin sacrifice to older men. And when I say older, I don't mean late 20s or early 30s or even later than that. I mean men in their late 40s and 50s. I think I gave a lot of them genuine pleasure. And I started to enjoy it.

A few years into this career I had as the toy of older men, I found a quote in Judith Thurman's resplendent biography of Colette that explained how I felt then exactly. When she was a very young girl, Colette married Willy, a much older man who enjoyed her thoroughly and masterminded the start of her writing career. We could all use a Willy! Colette wrote, "They are numerous, those barely nubile girls who dream of being the spectacle, the plaything, the erotic masterpiece of an older man."

Have people told you you were beautiful, and have you believed them? Does it matter why the other person says you're beautiful, as long as it gets said? Has anyone ever told you you were ugly? If you have heard both in your lifetime, which one is more believable? A man once told me I was "striking." That sounds about right. That can go either way, and going either way can be a pleasure. Suspense can be a pleasure.

I was raised in the Catholic church, so pleasure to me was something that needed to be paid for, but at least it was out in the open. In my life, I have often rejected the repressions of Protestantism, and not just because certain relatives in my Irish family would take me aside at family gatherings and tell me that the Catholic church was the one true faith and that the Protestants were stubbornly wrong and would come to no good once they had drawn their last pleasure-suppressing breath.

During the day, when I wasn't out drinking and getting my sexual if not sentimental education, I was watching videotapes from the red clock tower library on Sixth Avenue and 10th Street, which had once been a jail. Mae West had been booked there for obscenity in 1927. I also rented movies from TLA Video on 8th Street off Sixth Avenue, which was new and clean and well-lit and well laid-out and had a notably attractive staff. They grouped their videos by actor or actress, which suited me down to the ground then. It was only a dollar and sixty cents for each movie if you returned them before 6 PM, and so I was often shooting up and down Seventh Avenue around noon and then again at 5 PM or so.

Sometimes I would watch three movies in a row and then go out and have some kind of sexual contact with three or four guys, mainly jerking off. I always wore a black baseball cap when I went out like this, and I thought of this as my "Sex Hat." There were nights when I would stand in G Bar on 19th Street between Seventh and Eighth Avenue in the cream-colored circle around the bar that I called the Circle of Lust for hours and hours on end, looking to the left, looking to the right, and getting absolutely nowhere. The oldest, fattest, most repulsive men would outright reject me on nights like those. Well, this is what's called the luck of the draw, or is it the wages of sin?

Was I waiting for Ben Morrissey? Maybe I thought that if I couldn't have him that I might as well throw myself away on the most unsuitable and inappropriate guys, and very anonymously. All this random jerking off kept my love pure, ha ha. But then again, those sorts of guys were all I was able to find at that time, somehow. I often think about all the guys I would have met then if that generation of gay men hadn't been so decimated by AIDS.

The older guys that were left seemed shell-shocked. And some of them, mean as this is to say, were the guys that nobody wanted to sleep with to begin with. I know that sounds cruel, but who's to say I'm not one of those guys myself? I'm not in that category, I don't think, or not quite. I'm iffy, or I was. Which can be the cruelest thing of all. For if you're outright hopeless you can adjust to that, and early. But if you're iffy … you always wonder if this will be the night when someone will see you differently as a swan. You stay ready for that.

When I was sixteen, I went on a summer vacation with my parents. We went to a tropical location. I had secretly bought red "bikini underwear" at the mall, which I thought of as the height of sexiness then, in a *Melrose Place* sort of way. At night, I would sneak out of our hotel room and go to the beach and put the red bikini underwear on, and I would walk slowly back and forth on the cold sand as the waves came listlessly in.

I felt daring and naughty as I walked on the nighttime beach. The underwear was sexy. Maybe I was, too. Maybe the red bikini underwear would confer something like sexiness on me. I was totally and cosmically alone in the quiet and nothingness of that deserted beach, and I would wait to be seen, both expecting it and knowing that it would not happen. I did feel sexy or "sexy" but somehow exiled, beside the point, someone in solitary confinement singing to themselves only. I was alone and ignored even by the air and the sand and the water. This body! Here! Doesn't anyone want it? Wouldn't they?

During the summer, I would sometimes strip naked and go out and stand near our four-foot pool in the backyard and hope that someone was looking at me. I picture myself as a teenager always alone in this atmosphere of immense nothingness and standing nearly naked or naked and wanting so much to be seen, like a star in the black night sky. Did anyone see me on the beach or in the backyard? Probably not. Maybe God. But I don't think even God was all that interested.

So this prelude was why I was half-dead at nineteen but waiting to be revived. I was really just waiting to do Ben's bidding or to be of some help to him. Now that's love. Or you could say that I was clever enough to never ask too much of him, though I may have overstepped my bounds on occasion. If I did, Ben was too basically sweet to let me know about it. Do you still believe that Ben is nice? Ben is nice. He really is. Please keep that in mind during what comes next.

The editors and gallerists and art world people had all responded in one way or another to Ben's mass mailing, and he was showing in lots of group shows, and I went to all of them. Oh my, those were the nights of ten, eleven, twelve glasses of that wretched Sauvignon Blanc white wine that tasted like black pepper. You just had to swill it down quickly and try not to let the liquid touch your taste buds.

At Ben's place in Tribeca, which he shared with a bunch of other guys, fairly genial Wall Street pricks all of them, he always had a jug of red Carlo Rossi in his room that we (OK, *I*) would drain to the dregs, and "dregs" is a word that might have been invented for the—what is it? bits of sediment?— that you find at the bottom of a jug of Carlo Rossi. Ben said, "Your boyfriend Carlo Rossi," to me as often as possible.

We'd get to the gallery on the Lower East Side half smashed already (the galleries hadn't moved to Chelsea yet, and Ben has remained appealingly loyal to the Lower East Side for showing his work). I got to know the Art Types who frequented these things. Some of them had been going since the days of the Cedar Tavern and de Kooning on 10th Street. There was an old lady of maybe eighty so bent over from osteoporosis that she moved in a careful ninety-degree angle to the cheese and crackers, which were probably her only sustenance.

Ben started hanging around with a bunch of rich kids who did drugs and took lots of Polaroids of themselves shooting up in their underwear and having bad breath 6 AM fucks, and their collective work started to go over big in the art world, but Ben's was the best, his was set apart from theirs, and I don't just say that as someone who loves him. Critical cases have been made for him in the pages of *Artforum* and the like, and they will continue to be because he's the real thing. I knew it quite early, I felt it. He was sort of a rich kid himself, but not at the level of these kids.

I disliked them intensely right away, and my dislike hardened into implacable hatred as the years went on. One or two of the worst of them have since died, overdoses, and I wish I were a good enough Christian to say I forgive them, but I don't. After I'm crossed or insulted or what have you, I can wait years and years for an opening to pay back an unkindness. You bide your time, you bide your time, and then you insert the knife.

There began to be a lot of travel for Ben's work, but I didn't go. I wanted to stay in Manhattan. Ben and his buddies went to Rome a lot. The girls he saw started to get coarser, more confrontational, more insecure. They wore harsh make-up on their small faces and favored piercings and tattered black clothes. They tried to prove that they could drink and fuck just like any man. They made me uncomfortable. But when Ben started taking photos of them, his work got even more popular and gained more press. There came to be a certain "Ben Morrissey Girl," and his photos started to take on a rougher, more self-conscious edge, but they never lost their essential humanism. Or maybe I was just projecting what I felt about Ben onto them?

Ben had made a whooping proud deal about my losing my virginity finally, which took three or four tries at Rawhide to really be done properly but was never done properly for a while, in all honesty. To really lose your virginity, you have to yield to someone that you're in love with and take them and use them for your purposes, too, and that hadn't happened. Sex was just something I did then, and I was afraid of so-called social diseases, so it was almost all just groping and jerking. It had to be aligned to alcohol. I drank until I felt sexy, and so naturally I had to drink a lot.

The weird thing was, I was starting to get recognized in certain places as Ben Morrissey's favorite male model. I had become part of his publicity narrative and positioned as a kind of enigmatic gay guy mascot to Ben and his New York school photo crew. I was written about as enigmatic because I never knew what to say or how to position myself. Most likely I was excruciatingly self-conscious about my look and whatever persona I was trying on at the moment. It was assumed by many people that we were sleeping together, and Ben sometimes encouraged this idea, very slightly, but we weren't.

OK, so this is how certain things began. There was this prominent male art patron whose wife ran a gallery in Chelsea and knew everybody. Ben could profit from being friendly with the wife in no immediately tangible way but in many tiny ways, and she was difficult to get to, and eventually, through several drunken evenings, it was made clear to me that Ben was trying to get in with the wife through her husband the art patron. Ben would be flirtatious with him, talking all about his girls and making the guy laugh, and it was clear that the guy was excited by Ben and his sex talk.

He was a sharp-looking pale pencil of a guy, the kind whose suits never quite fit him, though he was very rich. He had the kind of thin, neat face that looked cruel, but that was only his look. He wasn't all that cruel, he was just a very distant and probably deeply unhappy man. Ben would get him so furtively excited with sex talk and then, gradually, he started telling this man about *my* sex life, and this man, OK, let's call him Arthur, suddenly got quiet and blushy. I could tell that he was attracted to me and wanted to hear about me having sex but he was basically shy, highly repressed.

Again gradually, with more meetings and more drinks, Arthur lost his shyness. In fact, when Ben would start telling him about the sex I was having (he always made it sound much more exciting than it actually was), Arthur would start to openly look me over and stare at my body. It was the summer of 1998, right before Antonioni and Monika Lilac, and I was wearing really tight shorts one night. We were drinking gin and tonics that Arthur was paying for. I was starting to play the role that had been given me by Ben.

I swung my left leg up over the arm of the chair I was sitting in so that my calf was spread out against it. My body is serviceable, sometimes more serviceable than other times when I'm working out a little, but my legs have always been my best feature. My legs are the one thing I've gotten compliments on consistently all through my relative youth.

I knew that Arthur would say, "You have really nice legs," which he did, and I knew that I would explain that my calves were so large because I did yoga every night at 6 PM, and that that would lead to talk about exercise, body talk. I glanced over at Ben and saw an expression on his face I'd never seen before, a kind of blank look. Was it a kind of blank ... expectant look? What was he feeling then? He never told me, then or afterward. But I'm sure he knew what I was doing, and that it needed to be done.

Arthur bought me lots of gin and tonics that night. He knew that I needed to be really drunk. He talked to me about the photos Ben took of me, and he was fairly blunt about what he liked about me in them. Arthur had a nasty streak, actually, and to be honest, it turned me on. If he'd been nicer or more sincere or more embarrassed, this whole thing might have been extremely unpleasant. But he wasn't, he was above board and more than a little crude, and as he kept talking about my body in the photos I shot one more split-second look at Ben and saw that he was slumped in his chair opposite us at the trendy bar we were in. His posture suggested something like defeat.

Arthur put his hand on my right knee, finally, and he didn't waste much time getting the hand higher and higher up my thigh and into my shorts. We were all really, *really* drunk now because for some reason Arthur had switched us to vodka tonics in tall thin frosted glasses, and this switch from gin to vodka was just lethal. Arthur was an uptight guy in his sober, married life, but with all this conflicting liquor in him he became a guy who felt no shame about groping my crotch in the middle of a crowded straight lounge at 10 PM or so on a Tuesday night. I was too drunk to have many feelings beyond the pleasure of a hand on me, any hand would do. I looked over at Ben. He wasn't in his chair anymore. Arthur stuck his tongue in my ear, and that was pretty gross, no question. He said something about me and Ben and everybody knew about us.

I shook my head and laughed. "I love him," I said. "But we don't do that." I got really upset instantly, in that turn on a dime drunken way, but Arthur didn't notice. He had both hands down my shorts now, one in front and one in back, and he was grabbing whatever he felt like grabbing. And then I turned on a dime again.

I was aroused by the fact that I was just a sexual object to Arthur, and not even a coveted object. In fact, I was merely an *intermediate* sexual object and link to Ben Morrissey, who wasn't about to put out for a guy, but hey, his little gay friend and model would, and so that made me valuable as a physical commodity. And I have to say, I liked all of this, as I realized it, and I especially liked the parts of it that should have been insulting to most people in this situation. Was I discovering just how perverse I could be, or was it a discovery of basic pragmatism, or was it both? Can pragmatism be borne out of perversity?

So Arthur now had his fingers in me and his gross wet tongue in my ear again. I assume people were looking at us. Arthur was one of those extremely repressed people who all of sudden behaved outrageously when their pent-up energy got to be too much to bear. I looked up and over again and Ben was back in his chair opposite us. He was staring straight at me with the tiniest little sad smile, and this smile of his made me almost insane with pleasure. This twisted situation was giving me all kinds of deep, intense vibrations of emotional and physical excitement.

We got the check, and Arthur never stopped mauling me for a second. When we tried to stand up, we all fell in a heap on the floor and had to be helped to the door, and I started to laugh, and Ben laughed a little, too, but just a little. I was just on fire, feeling wanted and degraded and loved and so happy.

We got in a taxi. This was one of many drunken times in my twenties when I got into the backseat of a taxi with an older man in a suit and stretched my legs out all over him so that I could be groped as much as possible. Ben sat in the front seat. He sat completely still. Very, very drunk and yet sober in himself. I stared at those huge shoulders of his and that powerful-looking neck and his curly hair. The curls were bigger and softer-looking now because it was so humid outside. We rode up Eighth Avenue to Arthur's little apartment on 29th Street. This little apartment he kept was much bigger, of course, than the apartments of people who had plenty of money but not tons of it.

There was the sound of keys being tossed on the floor. "He's mine," Arthur said. I remember that vividly, of course. Arthur didn't address that to me. He didn't say, "You're mine." He addressed it to Ben, who looked helpless and really, really angry now. In the confusion, I put my arms around Ben's neck for a second and said, "It's OK, really."

But was it? I was still actually a virgin in the final analysis. And with that go-right-ahead stupidity of ignorance, I took off all my clothes and got on the huge, plush bed in the back and looked at the high, high white ceiling and watched as Arthur took his clothes off. Erect and naked, he looked even more like a pencil than he did with his clothes on, but now he was an enraged pencil.

And … well, I don't know if I can possibly describe just how much it hurt. Suddenly Arthur's lack of consideration for me created a physical price that had to be paid. It was like being stabbed by fire over and over again, and I wasn't ready for pain like that. I couldn't get used to it. But I was so stupid and willing that in the midst of my panic and hurt I thought that I shouldn't *look* like I was in pain, I should try to look sexy. And so I threw my head to the side and tried to make groans that didn't sound like I was being stabbed or punched.

I looked up at Arthur. He had his eyes closed. Ben had always gone on and on about how he loved when a girl would dig her nails into his back during sex, and he would even show off the nail marks on his back with pride. And so I tried to dig my fingers into Arthur's back, but he snarled, "Spare me your nails," and so I stopped.

He didn't open his eyes. Was he thinking of Ben? Somebody else? Well, at least I didn't feel the need to act sexy anymore when I realized that Arthur wasn't even going to look at me. After probably the longest twenty minutes of my life, he stopped and pulled out and went into the kitchen. I just lay there, shocked and still drunken, but not nearly drunken enough.

"We're going to try doggie-style," Arthur said in the tone of someone ordering a coffee. I had no idea what that meant. Seriously. I was really sheltered then. I wanted to go, get out of there, but I couldn't. I'd already come this far. He impatiently ordered me on all fours when I didn't respond to his first Starbucks order, and he got in me again, and it was almost just as bad as before, but not quite. It was slightly less horrific.

I don't know if Arthur had his eyes closed at this point, but I remember that he started trash talking, and it sounded very silly. I know how hard it is to make dirty talk really land. It can so easily sound silly right away or, even worse, it can work really well for a little bit and then turn totally silly all at once. We were both pretty sweaty at this point, and Arthur started pulling my hair and ordering me to arch my back.

I didn't see Ben come in, but I knew he was in the room. I didn't want to look at him watching us, but I did look over to him as the hair pulling got rougher. All at once I was with Ben, outside of my body, just with Ben. We made eye contact, and it was *intense*. Wow, did he ever love me right then. I'm going to guess that this was the height of our love for each other, this moment. There were other moments, but none quite like this. He got across to me that he was somehow going to *fix* this situation. But I had no idea how until Ben walked over to the bed and slid both of his huge hands onto my chest.

He gave me a moment to assimilate the fact that he was touching me, and then his hands covered my tiny pectoral muscles and gently started to squeeze and knead them, as if I had breasts and Ben was touching them. It was exactly the way that he would have felt my upper body if I had been a girl with breasts. I was a boy, and he loved me, and so he translated that into touching me in this way. It wasn't as if he was pretending I was a girl, no, this was different. He was *relating* to me as if I was a girl, but I was still his Bobby, his best friend, his model, his confidante.

Arthur stopped what he was doing to me at some point and I'm pretty sure that Ben knocked his hand away very roughly when he tried to interact with us. I started to cry really, really hard, the kind of hard crying where you feel like your head is just going to split open. "C'mere, c'mere, c'mere," Ben whispered, grabbing all of me and creating this Ben Morrissey hug shield around my body. "I've got you, I've always got you, Bobby," he said. That made me cry even harder.

I don't know what Arthur was doing or what his reaction was. I didn't care at all then, of course, but I'm curious now. Was he ashamed? Turned-on? Repulsed? I don't know. He never told me. I assume that he retreated back into his most repressed persona and scurried away. I cried for a really long time, and Ben cried a little, too. We fell asleep like that in each other's arms. Maybe we're still there like that. I think there are moments in life when time really does stop moving forward, or time becomes like a mold around a perfect moment and lets it just rest for a little bit. Just rest for a little bit.

We were still in '90s sensitive guy mode then, so of course we talked and talked about our feelings for each other and talked around what had happened at lots of agonized and very enjoyable coffee binges by day and any-liquor-we-could-get-our-hands-on by night. My money was dwindling, but I was still solvent, and Ben seemed more than willing to buy every single one of my drinks. We were even closer now, but in a more relaxed way, as if some sort of pressure had been lifted. It was as if we had gone to bed together finally, but on our own totally fucked-up and co-dependent and unconventional terms. I started to take more interest in the women Ben was interested in, and this brings us back to Monika Lilac.

III

Ben and I were sitting in the upstairs theater at the Anthology Film Archives when he spoke her name as Monika Lilac sat down in her habitual spot, in the second row, center. He exhaled her name, actually, and the tone of his voice was almost completely silly, with none of his usual gravitas underneath, and this tipped me off right away that Ben had a thing for her so deep-rooted that he had to retreat behind a cartoon version of his feelings.

I asked him to spell her name, and he did. I said, "As in *Summer with*," and he asked me to explain more urgently. I said that it was the title of an Ingmar Bergman movie I had watched with headphones on the second floor of the Bobst Library at NYU. I had filled in almost all of Bergman and Jean-Luc Godard on the second floor of Bobst, and now the Anthology was filling in all of Antonioni (the only feature of his that they didn't wind up showing was *I Vinti*).

"It sounds like a stage name," I said, and Ben needed no further prompting to go into a low-voiced, impassioned recital of what he had been able to learn about Monika Lilac. He didn't know that her first name most likely came from a Bergman film ("Thanks, dude!" Ben said, bestowing a shoulder rub on me), but he had heard from a lady friend of hers that the Lilac came from the title of her favorite movie, *Lilac Time*. "Have you seen that, can you tell me something about it?" Ben asked, in an earnest, collegiate manner I had never experienced with him before.

I had no doubt now that this particular woman had got to him. I told Ben that I hadn't seen *Lilac Time*, but that I knew it was a silent romance of some sort with Colleen Moore and Gary Cooper. Ben knew Gary Cooper from *High Noon*, but even I'd never seen Colleen Moore in a movie. I explained that she had been a huge star in the 1920s, the first flapper, and that a film called *Flaming Youth* had made her a star. "Can we see that, can we see that and *Lilac Time*?" Ben asked, but I had to tell him that *Flaming Youth* was mainly lost, only a bit of it survived in an archive, and that *Lilac Time* wasn't easily viewable and that if we wanted it we'd have to get a bootleg tape from Grapevine Video or some such.

I glanced over at Monika sitting motionless up front, and I realized that I had seen her before at screenings. She was one of those repertory screening room people. She had a scent, something Parisian and expensive. (I found out later that Monika claimed she never wore perfume, but as with so many statements of hers, it was more a heartfelt position of some kind rather than an actual fact.) She was tall, maybe six feet, and stately.

She moved through space as if she had done those old-fashioned lessons that girls used to do where they walked around a room with a book on their heads. But sometimes her put-on regality broke open for a few moments and you noticed the loose, almost goosey sensuality of her movements, her generous breasts, which were versatile in that she would sometimes squeeze them up and together into a fetchingly heart-shaped décolletage, usually in winter, and in summer she just let them droop and swoop all over the place, à la Garbo.

Sometimes she wore enormous dark sunglasses indoors, the kind that used to be worn by Italian film stars in the 1960s. Ben said to me then that Monika reminded him of an Italian film star of that time, no one in particular, just the idea of an idea of a female Italian film star. Her hair was black and tight and curly, and it was sometimes problem hair in humid weather, so she had a discreet array of hats that she wore, always hats from the late 1920s. What are they called, cloques? Toques? She was usually dressed all in shades of black, but in summer she would sometimes don very dark shades of blue. She was the kind of woman who had obviously given a lot of thought to her look, her appearance, yet there was no rigidity to the Monika Lilac look. In fact, she was capable of making the most outlandish dress mistakes and she would carry them off in the spirit of fun.

Her fingers were as elongated and elegantly made as Ben's alabaster digits, but Monika was dark-complected, and in the summer her richly colored skin would become a sort of milky cocoa. There was a light dusting of little black freckles on her face. Some of them might have been drawn on for effect. Her nose was long and looked best in profile, and she certainly knew that. She was forever turning to profile (the left was best) and I don't think anybody got to see her full-face for more than a few seconds.

Her eyes were very unusual. I later found out that they looked so vivid because she lined them with kohl, which had been the favored eye make-up of Egyptian queens and certain silent film stars. She once tried to explain to me the process of applying kohl to her eyes, and it seemed complicated and somewhat dangerous, she had to burn it or something, but the effect, she explained, was worth it, and I had to agree.

Her lips ... well, Lord. They were perfection, the ideal shape, not too much, just enough. The lower lip in particular. She almost never put anything on them but a little lip gloss, though on rare occasions she would slash them with shocking 1940s fire engine red, but this was only for emergencies. Monika's black fan eyebrows obviously took a lot of time and care, but perfect beauty can take time, energy, effort.

Ben was Monika Lilac's opposite. He took pride in just rolling out of bed and being devastatingly sexy right away. I suppose you could say that Ben had natural beauty and Monika's beauty was mainly created through the force of her will and the selection of the proper material, the proper make-up, the proper lighting. No one knows or probably will ever know just exactly how old Monika Lilac is, but it's safe to say that she was a good ten years older than us then (we were twenty-one at the time).

Ben had been intrigued by Monika when he saw her vaporize at various film screenings I dragged him to. Monika never seemed to walk into a room but just seemed to appear, all of a sudden, which had the effect of startling you slightly, and so after making her mysterious entrance she seemed to seek to put you at ease, visually, with her slow, sinuous movements, the tilt of her head, the way her fingers caressed the air, the regality of her smile, which was one of those impenetrable smiles that functioned as a kind of armor or mask. It was a "dazzling" smile, blinding, like blaring sun bouncing off warrior shields, and it signaled: "Watch out!" Or be careful.

And so we watched *Cronaca di un amore*, in the worst print in the world. Afterward Ben and I lingered and watched Monika as she drew together her bag and her paper-thin black shawl and put on her enormous sunglasses. This was one of those times when the sunglasses didn't look silly on her and seemed just right. She floated out of the screening room, and we waited just a moment before we looked for her, but of course she had vanished. Where did she go? What did she do?

We went to B Bar to discuss Monika and our feelings about our feelings. That was where you went then in Manhattan, B Bar, on 4th Street between the Bowery and Broadway. And you had lunch at Balthazar, a French bistro on Spring Street where everybody stared at everybody else and you had to put on a performance of yourself. It was very theatrical. I could only manage it when I was drunk. Lots of champagne, lots of Campari and soda. Those were my drinks, what Louise Brooks might have called pansy drinks.

I could tell that Ben was not just intrigued by Monika but unsettled. Of course this intrigued me, so I started to make some inquiries into who she was or might be, and the information I gathered was sometimes disturbingly contradictory. Some people loved her, but a lot of people couldn't stand her. One thing was certain: Monika Lilac was obsessed with silent film, and she had obsessions within this obsession and all kinds of idiosyncrasies.

She loved Colleen Moore, the star of her favorite film *Lilac Time*, and she derided Louise Brooks as "common." Moore had been a huge star in the

1920s, whereas Brooks had been a snooty, red-hot also-ran starlet, at least in America, but their fame had reversed with the years, and now Brooks was widely known for her three European films and her film essays and her colorful self-destructiveness and the stable, pragmatic Moore, who had retired, made a lot of money on the stock exchange, and created an elaborate dollhouse that was a feature of a Chicago museum, had fallen into obscurity.

Monika had a whole website devoted to Moore, and another website devoted to the even more obscure Barbara La Marr, who had been known as "The Girl Who Is Too Beautiful." La Marr had died at age twenty-nine in 1926 of tuberculosis, but she had managed to marry four or five men by then before being too beautiful did her in. I pored over Monika's sites on the bedroom-filling computer I had bought for myself, which was state of the art then.

I had befriended a programmer at the Museum of Modern Art, and he had told me an off-color story about Moore hooking up with director King Vidor in the early 1970s when they were on the same floor of a hotel together—apparently it was a rekindling of a romance they had shared when they'd worked together on a film in the early 1920s. And so when Monika Lilac materialized at a screening of Antonioni's four-hour documentary on China, I felt that I had a piece of information that might interest her.

Ben was sitting next to me, and Lord knows it wasn't because he wanted to see Antonioni's China documentary but because he would take any and every opportunity to see Monika. I had never seen him like this over any woman. But maybe that was it. Because Monika was very much a woman, and not one of these girls who were always around and taking off their clothes for his camera and understanding, all of them, that he was not for settling down with on any level. There are lots of American girls who stay girls all their lives, and lots of boys who stay boys, and I never did find out where Monika was from, but she had a European quality about her that might have been natural or might have been partly or wholly manufactured.

This was extremely awkward, it really was, just excruciating, but I got up out of my seat and made my way to her row, where she was sitting by herself (even when the house was crowded, nobody ever dared to sit next to her or even around her if it could be helped), and I gently tapped her on the shoulder. Monika snapped her head around at me as if she had been shot, but she recovered herself quickly when I began to stammeringly tell her how much I loved Colleen Moore and Barbara La Marr and how much I loved her sites and the work she was doing for silent film.

She did the "dazzling" smile up at me and signaled that I should sit down, and I think that she gave me her hand and that I kissed it! I'm almost certain that happened, but the heat of my first encounter with Monika made me a little deranged, so I might be gilding the lily a little. Surely Monika would approve, as the ultimate lily gilder of all time, or at least our time then, in our set.

Then I made a mistake. I rushed into telling Monika the elderly sex dirt about Moore and King Vidor, and I told it badly, I'm sure, and the smile slowly collapsed, as if invisible little hands had pried it down off her face and thrown it against a wall with great force. At a certain point, she held up her manicured hand, which signaled that she couldn't stand to hear any more, and then she turned away from me and stared up at the screen expectantly.

The audience was over, and I realized right away the mistake I had made. So much of Monika's feeling for Moore was as a corrective to the promiscuous Louise Brooks, as the original flapper sweetheart, as someone who had walked away from the movies and led a happy, productive, interesting, rather conservative life. Monika saw the ascension of Brooks over Moore in the pantheon of silent film stars as a sign of declining standards, perversity, and destructiveness. Even at the time, I felt that this was a pretty wacky point of view when I read over her feverish, obscure prose on her Moore and La Marr websites. But I've always liked extreme people with extreme positions, even if I can't agree with them.

I slunk back to my seat and told Ben that I had failed, and I tried to explain why. A lot of other guys would have been mad at me, or would have been mad but pretended poorly that they weren't, but that wasn't Ben's way. I explained the situation in detail, and he just nodded and felt bad for me. "Thanks for trying, man, you're the best," he said.

I suppose you could say that I had an incentive to set myself up to fail just so that I could receive the sympathetic responses of Ben. You can look at certain situations in the harshest possible light, or you can be more charitable. Either slant might be true. But I'm a Catholic, so I feel that being as hard on yourself and on the situations you find yourself in is best. You can always pull back later. It's like rehearsing a play. You can always go big and then have the director pull you back down to earth. Get it over with, look at things harshly. Once you do, and you pull back, you find that something like grace might enter your life. If the grace of God is a mirage, then it's still the best we have.

We sat through the first two hours of the China documentary, and I was enthralled, but I could tell that Ben was in an agony of boredom, twisting his super-tall body this way and that in his seat until I just decided to enjoy his physical discomfort. To get through some situations, it helps to be perverse. Besides, there's nothing more erotic to me than sitting in the dark of a movie theater right next to someone you desire. It's so intimate, like you're dreaming together, inside each other's bodies, inside each other's heads. The lights went up for intermission, and Ben stopped moving for a moment and looked expectantly over at Monika, who was just sitting there unmoving, her face uptilted as it always was. It was as if she were in a trance.

We stood to stretch our legs, moving subtly closer and closer to where Monika was sitting. Finally, Ben got up the courage to go over and introduce himself, and the smile came back out in full force for him. I sidled over behind Ben, and when Monika saw me the smile grew particularly blinding. "Oh darling, come here and sit down, I'm sorry I was so rude!" she said, and so I sat down next to her and Ben towered over us and so we began.

"There's no excuse for rudeness, not even when an illusion is ripped from us," she said. I remember she clawed the air with one of her expressive hands when she said, "ripped." Ripped from us with sharp Jungle Red fingernails, torn to pieces. "But listen, I've been thinking about it, and Colleen had a deep, *deep* feeling for King, and they had a romance of sorts when they were filming *The Sky Pilot* in 1921, and so of course she would want to rekindle that, revisit that! Who am I to judge? Who am I to comment?"

I said something about loving the idea of older people having sex, that it gave me hope, and Monika's face tightened slightly. "I'm not old enough to know yet," she said and uncorked her phenomenal laugh. Some people have laughs that are just obtrusive, and it's as if they were born with them, they just can't help it. Loud honks, or hollow shouts, or tiddly little giggles (that would be me, I'm afraid). Monika's laugh was so unnerving because it was so studied. It had obviously been worked on and it seemed to be a copy of not just one laugh but several that she had appropriated and put together until, presto!, she had the unmistakable Monika Lilac laugh.

I suppose it was the sort of laugh that you could call "rippling," and it was redolent of a certain kind of theatrical leading lady of the 1920s or early '30s, like Ina Claire or Ruth Chatterton. It was a dated laugh. It was like something that you couldn't put your finger on. It was meant to provoke, disturb, give pleasure. Monika's laugh was the height of artificiality, and it was a kind of triumph, but it was like the smile, watch out!

When Ben decided to sit down on my lap, this made Monika let out the laugh a second time, even louder. I could see that some of the people still in the theater were giving her dirty looks. Some had long experience of

Monika and her smile and her laugh and her haughty, peremptory manners, and she inspired much ambivalence in the revival house crowd.

Ben got all touchy-feely with me, and she laughed even more. This seemed to really delight her. The way Ben had of physically mauling and loving me in public always, *always* got a girl attracted to him, and this act even worked with a difficult woman like Monika. When her laugh died down, Ben laid his large curly head on my right shoulder, very tenderly, and Monika reached over and began to stroke the back of his neck, as she would have stroked a particularly sexy cat (Monika was the cat-lover of cat lovers, of course).

"Do we have to see the rest of this?" Ben asked in a slightly whiny voice. It was the voice of a favored male child who always gets his way no matter what. No one ever said no to Ben. I couldn't either, even though I was dying to see the rest of Antonioni's China film, which the Anthology's catalogue rightly called "the rarest of the rare." But Monika solved this dilemma.

"You go and get yourself a drink or whatever it is that you get, and Robert and I will stay and finish the film, and we'll meet you outside in two hours. How's that?" she asked. That was fine, of course, and now it was my turn to laugh when Ben smiled his goofiest smile and bounded out of the screening room like a freed prisoner. "He's unusually attractive, but he isn't one of us, is he?" Monika asked. I asked what she meant. "He isn't a cinephile," she said. That was the first time I had heard that word. A cinephile—is that what I was? I was always watching movies as a kid and as a teenager. That's practically all I did. Now it had a name.

We sat through the rest of the documentary together and I breathed in her perfume that wasn't supposed to be perfume. There was such a powerful stillness about her presence when she was really concentrating on the images in front of her, and something very childlike, too, something very "tell me a story." There were some walkouts, but we were mainly among hardcore Antonioni fans, and this was a holy grail at that time, before digital downloads started to make practically everything available if you knew where to look and you didn't mind operating outside the laws of copyright.

When it was over, Monika just sat there in her seat for a few moments, unmoving, and then she started to come back to life again, slowly, as if a spell had been broken. I thought of myself as a film enthusiast or buff at that time, but in Monika's presence, and under Monika's influence, I started to become what she had called me, a cinephile, a member of a smallish religious cult with different factions, rules, customs, viewpoints, and habits.

I asked her what she had thought of the film, and she waved her hand at me, fairly warmly but firmly, as if to say, "Too soon!" It was my first lesson in true cinephilia. You don't ask someone what they thought of a film right away. It's rude and crass, and it likely kills the real response that is forming after the lights come up. We rose out of our seats and she linked her arm in mine as we walked down the stairs to the lobby and out onto 2nd Street, where Ben was patiently waiting for us.

His expression was very "I have been patiently waiting for you," and it made Monika do a semi-Ina Claire ripple laugh as she linked her other arm in his. We didn't say anything to each other but just walked like that west on 2nd Street into Greenwich Village. Monika was leading us, because she was a leader. Monika was something of a martinet, and you went where she led you.

As we sat down in a sidewalk café, the Caffe Reggio on MacDougal Street with those enormous oil paintings inside, Monika ordered a bottle of rosé wine and told us that she only drank rosé in the summer. I offered that I mainly drank Campari and soda in summer. Monika's face lit up and she clasped my hand and cried, "Oh, you're one of those!" I smiled uncomfortably. But it seemed vaguely complimentary, and so I let my misgivings go.

Ben asked her what she had thought of the film. Some time had passed, and so she didn't wave his question away. Then again, she might not have dismissed his question if he had asked her in the theater. Monika Lilac had the strictest cinema-going rules of anyone, but even she might have broken them for Ben. "I've never seen so many faces that told me absolutely nothing," Monika said, in a soft voice. "If China does take over the world, it's going to be a very … orderly place." She was very beautiful in the dim light coming from the café, in half profile. Monika could have recited her multiplication tables and it probably would have sounded seductively right to us. A beauty is most beautiful at the Caffe Reggio.

We talked in sweet nothings for a bit until we got into our wine, and the subject of romance came up. I remember Monika saying, "I feel that paradise is an attainable thing if you watch enough Josef von Sternberg films in the right frame of mind, preferably in chronological order, from 1925 to 1953."

Ben nibbled around the edges of the topic of romance for a bit, not wanting to scare Monika. She gave you the impression that she might bolt like a frightened animal if anything even remotely crude was said in her presence. Monika clearly lived in a world of her own creation, and if you wanted to visit it and become a part of it, you had to follow her rules. You couldn't confront her directly about anything, but that didn't mean that she was unable or unwilling to be lightly confrontational herself, to provoke, to stir things up, to give pleasure.

When Ben paused for a moment, Monika leaned forward slightly so that her breasts almost swung out of her black top and she clasped my hand hard. "How much do you love him?" she asked me. Not "Do you love him?" or "You must love him very much," or something like that. No, Monika assumed the love and she leapt right to something more important. How much do you love him?

Monika never looked you directly in the eyes but always seemed to focus on your right earlobe when she talked. Most cinephiles are not fans of eye contact. She asked me how much and stared intently at my right earlobe and waited for an answer. I wanted to answer honestly, but I also was calculating just what kind of answer would do Ben some good. I guess you could call that being a good friend.

In the few seconds I had to formulate a response, I thought of saying something non-committal, something flip, something sincere but guarded. Instead, though, I said, "I would give my life for him." Was it true? Yes, I think so. Because I loved life, but I loved Ben Morrissey more.

I looked at Monika and her face had a worried, maternal expression on it. It looked as if she were in pain, maybe. Her forehead creased, and suddenly she looked much older. There was a flash of doubt, a moment when all her armor collapsed. But only a moment. She said, "That's wonderful to hear, but are you really being sincere?" I said yes, right away. At that, she took a sharp intake of breath.

We both glanced at Ben, who was giving us a sheepish look. Monika got up very abruptly from the table, and she kissed us both lightly on the mouth and lightly tossed back the rest of her rosé from her glass. "I'm sure I'll be seeing both of you again," she said. She gathered up all of her fussy things and floated off as quickly as possible toward Washington Square Park. I wondered out loud where she lived. Ben wondered if she lived alone, and what she did for a living.

We drank a lot that night, and Ben was very touchy-feely with me, as if I were Monika, maybe, or as if I were a key that would open that particular door. The next day, I dug out my old Foothill Video catalog and looked for *Lilac Time*, but when I called I found that Foothill had gone out of business, and so we had to resort to Grapevine Video for a copy of it.

"How long do we have to wait?" Ben asked, all excited. He wanted a copy of this movie like *right now*, and I did everything I could to expedite it, but Grapevine was a poky company and it took several days before we were able to settle down after a night of drinking to watch *Lilac Time* at 6 AM or so. That's when Ben and I did all our viewing of this and that, when the sun was starting to come out. It wasn't a very good movie. In fact, it was bewilderingly pedestrian. All hearts and flowers and romance and such, and Gary Cooper was extremely beautiful, Ben and I both agreed.

But Colleen Moore mainly stuck to expressions of wide-eyed surprise and a standard, misty, looking-off-into-the-distance thing that was necessary for when Gary was off fighting the war. We had no idea why *Lilac Time* was Monika's favorite movie, even after poring over and dissecting her long essay on it on her Moore website.

Moore had donated her personal prints of her movies to the Museum of Modern Art because she wanted them to be preserved. Some of the studios wrote to the museum and asked for the prints. They said they owned them, you see. And so the Museum sent some of the prints back. And they were neglected, and a lot of them disintegrated. When Moore realized what had happened as an older woman, she was said to be heartbroken.

I'm not a fan of hers, but my heart goes out to her. She wanted her life's work preserved, and the studios only wanted what they owned, and then they let what they "owned" rot and disappear. That's greed and misguided, absent authority. Somebody needs to be in charge, but it's so rarely the right person. Monika said to me once, "Some silent films are so old that nobody owns them now. Or nobody wants them? Is there a difference?" And then she let out that laugh.

Monika's sites have long since vanished from the Internet, and they would probably seem crude now, visually, and I can't remember too much more of what she wrote aside from the bit about the way some of Moore's films were lost, but I do think she wrote a lot about silent romance, and how all romance should be silent. I don't agree with her.

"So who are you seeing?" Ben asked me, and I told him about the two or three older guys who were paying me court or calling me regularly. Ben tried to find this amusing, but he kept frowning at me, too. "Bobby, sweetie-pie, you deserve better," he said, finally. "What is it, don't you think you're good-looking enough for a guy your own age?" I let that question just hang in the air. I couldn't answer it.

I felt sleepy. I wanted to sleep in Ben's arms again. But he got up and poured us some more drinks. "C'mon, let's go online and find you a guy," he said. I had never done that before, and it was different then. There were chat rooms, and there weren't photos and profiles yet. It was pretty primitive.

Of course naturally I gravitated more toward the older guys who wanted to come over instantly to get a nice twenty-one-year-old than any of the actual twenty-one-year-olds who might have been in the chat rooms. Ben got increasingly frustrated with me. He wanted a perfect lover for me *right now*, and of course that wasn't likely to happen in a chat room at 8 AM or so on a Monday morning. And so he did what he could. "Take off all your clothes, even your socks, pretty boy," he said, in his goofy low voice. "Let's take some shots."

These weren't just any shots. Ben worked with me all morning. He took Polaroids, which was his standard practice then, but he also took some with a regular camera, with black and white film. I'm still hopelessly dense about cameras, but I do know that Ben did as much as he possibly could technically with a few different cameras in my apartment in natural light and then artificial light and then he told me to throw on a coat and we went outside and near the water and found deserted spots by the West Side Highway where I could briefly drop the coat and be naked.

I was hard, of course, and Ben said he wanted to take frontal shots of me, but I couldn't be hard for those. I couldn't get my erection to go down, and we were giggly about that, and finally Ben said, "OK, pretty boy, get down on all fours," in a really fantastically sleazy voice that I can still hear in my head. I did what he said to do. Ben put down his camera and spit in both hands, and as quickly and roughly and wonderfully as possible he was jerking me off really hard and fast. "Don't ever tell anybody we did this," Ben said, and I moaned and laughed, and I wanted this to go on forever, of course, but I was conscious of not making Ben wait too long, and this consciousness made me freeze up a little. I couldn't finish.

We were outside, we could have been caught, and that added to the excitement. "Stand up," he said, finally, and I did, and I wobbled a little bit from being lightheaded and scared and happy, and there was sunlight in my eyes, and I could hear cars going by all around us and the sounds of guys unpacking trucks nearby, and suddenly Ben was coming at me and taking his shirt off in like a split second, and he put his hands all over me and licked me weirdly and was kind of rough, and I laughed really loud, because his style of lovemaking with me was so eccentric. He put his left hand over my mouth and flipped me around and jerked me with his right hand until I finished, and he smeared the stuff all over my face and chest and then maneuvered me gently to the ground and grabbed his camera and took as many shots of me as possible stretched out like that on the cold corrugated metal platform we were on.

Those became famous photos later. I never told anyone how Ben got me to look like that. How he got those particular expressions of total insane bliss on my face. It all took just a few minutes. Three minutes? Four? Stolen moments.

Ben pulled me up from the ground fast and rudely when we were done, which made me laugh some more, and he threw the coat over me, and he must have known we were close to trouble because he said, "Run." We did, both of us laughing, and a guy far behind us was shouting, "I'm going to call the police! I'm going to call the police!" Well, call them! The police can't do anything, man. I think that's what Ben said then. It became a "story," so he might have said it, he might have said something like it, or it might have just been a pure invention for our publicity narrative. In any event.

As we walked downtown, Ben put his arm around me and said, "You know, if I was a gay guy, we would totally be together."

I said yes, sure.

"I wish girls had hard-on trouble and needed that particular treatment!" he said. The sun was shining on his curls and his trapezoidal mouth as he smiled. We were walking down Eighth Avenue.

"What, you never do it with your girl models?"

"Well, yeah," Ben said, "but girls need to be treated with more, I don't know, caution?"

"Respect?" I offered.

"Oh please, respect," Ben said.

"Respect is something a woman in love can't afford," I said in a serious voice.

"Girls," Ben said, dreamily, as if he hadn't heard me. "Monika will never pose for me, will she?"

"No," I said. "That's why you love her best. That's why I love you best, whatever."

"Whatever," Ben agreed.

Monika worshiped the film director Frank Borzage, who made many of the best romantic movies, and so we were certain that she would have to be at a Film Forum screening of Borzage's *A Farewell to Arms*. Film Forum was off Sixth Avenue and Houston Street, and it mainly did repertory screenings, and it had the best popcorn. Small screens, but fairly comfortable seats that had names on the backs of them of people who had donated money to make those self-same seats sittable. Sure enough, there Monika was, sitting in her seat in the center close to the screen, surrounded by a few girls who seemed to be admirers, even acolytes.

Monika was holding forth in her lightest, huskiest voice: "I don't see why they have to talk, but still and all, there's no more romantic shot in cinema than the image of Gary walking next to Helen Hayes ... he towers over her! I declare, her head only reaches his waist practically. Oh, Gary!" That "I declare" was an odd choice, because it made Monika sound for a moment like she was from the South, but maybe she had just seen a movie with a Southern heroine earlier in the day, or maybe one of her girls was from below the Mason-Dixon line. "I'm so suggestible," she confessed to me once.

She saw us and she nodded pleasantly in our direction, but her face took on a cloudy, humid expression. The lights went down and we watched the film, which really is one of the most beautiful of all time, and in the version they were showing Helen's Catherine Barkley died (there are some prints where it's suggested she might live, why not?).

After it was over, we took a moment to collect ourselves, and slowly approached Monika, who turned to us with tears in her eyes. This was unnerving, mainly because it looked as if they were false tears, as if they were glycerin that she had somehow applied to her face. The water hung below her eyes like large pearls and took quite a time to slide (whoosh!) dramatically down her cheeks. They seemed to be coming from the *center* of her eyes. It was a little like those statues of the Virgin Mary who weep in church alcoves, but maybe that's just me being Catholic.

I don't think she said, "Don't speak!" but she didn't have to. We knew not to, and she would have been able to get away with that line without getting a laugh. It was clear to me from the open expression on his face that Ben just loved everything about Monika, and I was fascinated by her, but ambivalent.

What I loved about Ben was that he was so splendidly straightforward. Monika made a production out of everything, so that every moment was a kind of fan dance or shell game. When a bit of self-deception crept into Ben's talk with me, he would immediately shoot it down himself as if an illusion based in ego couldn't possibly be sillier. For Monika, self-deception was her art, and when you got to know her it was like entering a maze. You didn't know where reality began and where her inventions would leave you off. Her conception of herself was Byzantine, and full of traps.

We walked out with her and aimlessly walked toward the water, and then we drifted up toward where Ben and I had quasi-hooked up and taken our photographs. Finally she said, "You know, sometimes I don't know the difference between looking at the screen and … looking at the screen, I don't know the difference." I wanted to help her, so I said, "Do you need to know the difference?"

Her face got childish and wide-eyed for a moment and then it hardened into surety so that she could announce, "No, it makes no difference," with authority (she could make transitions like a great actress). Ben huddled close to her, and he asked her to pose for him. I knew he had made a mistake. He was too impulsive, it was too early, and sure enough, she shot him down: "I do the looking," she said with an edge of disdain.

"Would you take pictures of me then?" Ben asked, taking his camera from around his neck and reaching out to her with it. Monika flinched from it as if he was about to hit her. "No, please, let's just walk a little more."

And so we did. We walked close to my apartment, and then all at once she smiled and laughed and said, "You know, I'm giving a party soon. It's going to be a special party, and I'd be delighted if you two boys would come." We said we'd love to come to her party, and so she asked for our addresses. She would be sending out formal invitations later in the week. Goodbye! And then she slipped away down Eighth Avenue, disappearing into all the guys parading to the gym or to Rawhide or to the pharmacy or to the Big Cup coffee shop for coffee and cruising.

We got super drunk that night at Peter McManus, the only real straight bar in Chelsea, on 19th Street and Seventh Avenue. Ben fell into a blue mood under the influence of too many two-dollar pints of Rheingold. He started asking me all sorts of questions about the mechanics of sex between guys, and he couldn't hide his disgust. "Guys are so *hairy*," he kept repeating. But he snapped out of it and got all laughy-touchy-feely again. I told him that one of my life's ambitions was to be crowned Miss Rheingold, and Ben couldn't get enough of that. He called me Miss Rheingold sometimes.

IV

The invitations from Monika arrived, and they certainly were formal. They might have been engraved, and if they weren't they looked as if they were. The *idea* of engraved invitations, she had that down pat with whoever did them for her. One of her girls, one of her acolytes, probably. The address was a brownstone on Washington Square Park. Could this be where she lived? We wondered that. The attire called for was formal, black tie, and so Ben and I went to the trouble of renting suits, but the invitation also said that some attire would be available at the party.

The party was called *7th Heaven*, and it had a photo of Janet Gaynor resting in Charles Farrell's arms set in the center and fading away from the text. The invitation made it clear that there was no talking aloud at this party. It was one of Monika's silent film parties. If you needed to make yourself understood, you would have to do so by pantomime, and if you really needed to speak, you would have to write your words down on intertitle cards that would be on certain tables in the house.

We gulped two glasses of flowery white wine at Ben's place before we went up to the house on Washington Square, and when we arrived we saw soft colored lights set around the staircase outside and all kinds of people quietly entering. A phonograph by the door was playing a scratchy record of John McCormack singing "Jeannine, I Dream of Lilac Time." His voice drifted slowly and almost inaudibly around the white steps and blended with the clicking of high heels. The women and girls were dressed in thrift store fashions that charmingly tried for either 1920s glamour or 1920s sweetheart-dom. Some of them obviously only had a vague idea of what they were doing, but everyone wanted to please Monika and create something with her, so any missteps with make-up or headgear were easily forgiven.

It was one of those old houses with only faint electricity, a nineteenth century Dutch house that seemed to be all hallway and staircase and striped wallpaper. Even if people had been talking or laughing, the walls would have soaked up the sound, and now they soaked up all the careful silence. Ben and I entered several different rooms and heard only the clickety whir of a projector playing various films on large screens.

In one room they were showing *My Best Girl* with Mary Pickford.

We looked at that movie for a while, and the more I stared at Pickford's leading man, Buddy Rogers, with his thick black hair and long eyelashes and pretty face, the hornier I got. Some people were trying to communicate in pantomime, and a lot of the girls were doing hoyden type acting work, with bulging eyes and frantic energy, as if they had seen some Clara Bow movies. The men were more reticent.

I left Ben alone and slipped back out into the hall and saw two men dressed as doughboys. They were maybe in their early thirties, and they were both super-cute. Before I knew it, I was playing out a scene with them where one of them was dying on the field (an airplane mishap?), and suddenly we were all kissing each other on the mouth! The wonderful thing was that we didn't get lascivious about it. We kissed each other just the way Buddy Rogers seemed to kiss Richard Arlen in *Wings*. We kissed without the awareness of any sexual connotation between men, like they did. Deeply hot, unaware kisses.

Finally Monika tapped my shoulder with her black fan and gave me the Smile of Smiles, and I embraced her gently. She seemed delighted to see me, and so I responded in kind. We pantomimed our delight for a while, and Monika took me by the hand and led me over to a small circular table by a park-facing window where she picked up one of her inter-title cards and wrote, "Is he here?" I nodded yes. Monika looked at me and mouthed, "Love never dies," as distinctly as Colleen Moore does at the end of *Lilac Time*, so distinctly that no inter-title was needed. This was Monika in her element. Monika's persona never quite worked when she talked, but in silence at her silent movie parties she was supremely attractive, a flickering image giving warmth and hope.

I gestured to where I had left Ben, and she took her leave of me with a smaller smile that displayed all the genuine warmth she had in her. She wafted away, and I went to explore some other rooms, some other films. John Gilbert was professing his love to a dying Lillian Gish in one room in *La Bohème*, and in another room he was scooped up by Greta Garbo in *Flesh and the Devil*.

Monika was a great proponent of John Gilbert. She often told the story of how Gilbert was stood up at the altar by Garbo and how he punched MGM chief Louis B. Mayer in the face after he made a "crude remark," which she never specified (Mayer had told Gilbert that he didn't need to marry Garbo, he could always just fuck her). And so Mayer, she would relate, ordered sound engineer Douglas Shearer (Norma's brother) to turn up the treble for Gilbert's debut sound film, *His Glorious Night*, in which his repeated cries, "I love you! I love you!" had audiences roaring.

"Imagine laughing at John Gilbert saying those words!" Monika would cry. "And so what did they get? James Cagney. Romance was out!" Sometimes Monika did sound like Norma Desmond, even though she always said she "couldn't stand" Gloria Swanson.

In another room the projector was unspooling *Beau Brummel,* with John Barrymore and Mary Astor. They fell in love while they were making that movie, and I could tell, even before Monika told me about it. *Beau Brummel* is mainly just the two of them staring at each other across rooms with burning eyes, and as I watched it, I started to go into a kind of silent romance trance. I started to feel that talking truly was unnecessary. How many parties would be so much better without all the small talk, with just bodies moving through space and glances and images unsteadily quivering on screens and walls all around you.

I left the *Beau Brummel* room after a while and tried to find my doughboys. They weren't in the *My Best Girl* room, but Ben and Monika were, and they were engaged in some dreamy pantomime, slow and shy, something very private. I wandered upstairs and paused to watch two young-looking girls professing love to each other and scribbling furiously on the inter-title cards and indulging themselves in a chaste kiss.

In the back room of the second floor, I spotted my doughboys staring up at a film of a woebegone lady in a large dress, viewed from some distance (I found out later that it was Norma Talmadge, a major, forgotten star of the 1920s, and one of Monika's pets). The taller of my doughboys beckoned me over to them, and I slipped in between them, so naturally, like water, and watched the lady on the screen.

We were the only ones in this room. It wasn't a particularly crowded party, and there were so many rooms, so many films. My doughboys put their hands on me gently. Their hands were tender and reflective, not at all like the invasive hands I was used to at bars in Chelsea like G and Rawhide. Their hands were exploratory, insistent, too. They sought to put me at ease, but they made clear that they wanted me.

We sunk down to the floor, fairly gracefully, and we watched the lady in her period dress preparing to see a beau. My doughboys ran their hands all along my body and cuddled me. It was highly sexual precisely because there was no outright sexual touching. We stayed like that for a long while, in a trance-like state, and finally we fell asleep for a bit, all entangled with each other, with only the sound of the projector clickety-clacking and the similar clicking of the women's heels in the halls on the hardwood floors.

I woke to another hand, a female hand, and I knew it was Monika. She was staring down at us with an amused, mask-like face, and she beckoned

DAN CALLAHAN

with her stringy arms for us to get up, which we did. It was as if we were underwater, and we moved in a woozy way, and this made Monika throw her head back and laugh silently. She was extremely beautiful in this artificial environment that she had created, so beautiful that I reached out and touched her face for a moment, because I felt like I could, and she accepted my touch happily, her face opening up like a flower. When this happened, her face changed drastically and suddenly something endearingly awkward was revealed about her, something gawky and adolescent. It was a glimpse of a private Monika, or maybe a girlhood Monika before she took on her name.

It had started to rain heavily, and there were crashes of thunder, but this didn't break the mood of her party, it enhanced it. Call me corny, but there's nothing more romantic than a thunderstorm. It was an electrical storm, and the leaves in Washington Square Park were being whipped here and there as Monika took my hand off her face and led me out of the house. We stood on the sidewalk in the rain for a bit. Two or three of Monika's girls were bringing the phonograph back into the house.

Monika's face was upturned into the rain, and it made an absolute mess of her make-up, and when she turned to me her eyelashes were comically askew and her curly hair was a disaster and her dress was being drenched and sticking to her body, so that her large breasts looked out of proportion to her torso, but she opened up her arms to the rain slowly. She bent down swiftly and started to unlace her complicated shoes and then she had them off and she plopped down on the ground and rolled off her silk stockings with the seams in back. She started to prance barefoot and bare-legged up and down the street. I took my shoes and socks off and joined her, and we laughed and got wetter than wet and held on to each other in the rain, which was coming down in sheets now and buffeting us around.

When we got back to the house we danced in through the door, and most of the guests were staring at us, as if waiting for a cue. Monika slipped over to the circular table by the door and scribbled something onto one of the inter-titles and ran to the midway point of the staircase so that everyone could read it. In large capital letters, it read: "Strip down to your underwear and take off your shoes and socks and fold your nice clothes and put them on the large oblong table in the Norma Talmadge room."

There was a moment of hesitation, and a few of the men looked especially uncertain, but then all of the girls started to scamper up the stairs and the men followed slowly behind them. My doughboys made a sharp move right for me and clasped both of my hands and pulled me willingly up the stairs, where we all undressed excitedly. I shyly glanced at my doughboys' long, slender bodies as they undressed (very Gary Cooper, both of them, I thought, and very Ben, too) and saw that they were wearing red long underwear with a trapdoor in back, and I was so turned-on by the sight of them in this particular underwear and embarrassed that I was wearing the then-popular boxer briefs and not period underwear.

They slipped their arms around my waist and we went back downstairs, where everyone was waiting. Monika was in very intricate and arousing black underwear, slightly bent over at the table by the window again, scribbling. She practically flew back up the staircase and held out an inter-title that read, "Go out into the rain and run around the block!" and quickly she held up another that read, "Whoopee!" There were huffy intakes of breath from the men and the girls were holding in squeals of delight.

We all streamed out into the night and ran like crazy, and the rain was really coming down now, thudding in big brutal drops on the sidewalk. My doughboys kept lifting me up in between them and I laughed soundlessly and the rain rushed into my mouth and I choked slightly and my head hung to the right on one doughboy shoulder, and then to the left on the other doughboy shoulder, and we were on Sixth Avenue now.

Some people were fighting the rain in their umbrellas, but they didn't pay us any mind. I sensed right away in Manhattan that you can look as weird as possible on the street, or talk to yourself, or do all manner of eccentric things, and no one will pay you any attention. I loved that at this point, when I was rushing through the night in my boxer briefs with a bunch of other people in period underwear.

In any other place, we might have been harassed, arrested, or the object of wide-eyed stares. Not in Manhattan. And that has its flip side, too. Because Manhattan will let you do whatever you like, at any time of the day or night, but it won't ever pay attention to you. You can be world famous, and Manhattan still basically doesn't care, most of the time. And if you aren't world famous, Manhattan regards you at several ice-slicked levels below indifference. And sometimes, on less wonderful days and nights, some attention might be welcome.

We got back to the house somehow, and there was a price to be paid. We were all shivering when we got inside, and we didn't know what to do next, and Monika wasn't around. And a small girl had stepped on a piece of glass, so that the sole of her right foot was nastily torn, and people were trying to find her some iodine and so forth, and they were talking. The spell was broken. The party was over.

I looked for Ben, and he wasn't around either. I figured that he and Monika were getting better acquainted. So I found my doughboys, who were holding their clothes and mine, and they put their arms around me and brushed the rain off me (so hot!) and smiled at me and one of them hailed a taxi (the rain had entirely stopped) and we sped off to their apartment deep in the East Village, in the area I knew as Alphabet City, which was supposed to be dangerous, but wasn't really, not anymore, not in 1998. We made love all night, in the dark. And we didn't say a word. Why not turn out the lights, when there is nothing more to be seen?

I snuck out in the morning before they woke up. I guess I didn't want them to act polite and make me breakfast and tell me about their polyamorous open relationship, or whatever. I just wanted them to be my doughboys and a mystery. It was September by then, I think, maybe even October, and it was still very warm. I went and had some eggs and toast and coffee at Cafe Orlin on St. Marks off Second Avenue, which was fast becoming my favorite café. Tanya had taken me there and now it was my place.

It was always lit dimly and had one of those low ornately designed tin ceilings. Cafe Orlin was a place for either intimate conversation or reverie. You could even, if you wanted, bring a book and while away an afternoon. I sat under the Brassaï photo on the wall near the front, the one of the man staring at an ecstatic-looking woman's face. That was my spot.

I treated myself to an almond tart with a second cup of coffee after I was done with the eggs. The food was good at Cafe Orlin, but the atmosphere was better. What a happy morning that was.

V

I began going to film screenings and reviewing new films for various start-up websites, and so I was able to take Monika to some things, but she always disliked the new movies and insisted on "cleansing our palettes" at another theater playing some old romance or other. She moved in with Ben, and this was done fairly casually. Monika didn't seem to own any furniture, only an elaborate wardrobe, some of which, she told me, was in storage. I could just imagine the peacock headdresses and the gold beaded gowns! Monika and Ben would be on the couch together for hours, just cuddling constantly, and I would make them dinner if the amiable Wall Street pricks weren't around, and they usually weren't. Those were quiet evenings.

The only time there was any tension is when Ben would ask Monika to pose for his camera, and she got more and more adamant that she would never pose for him. She said that still photos made everyone dead, or something like that, and that she needed to move or be moving at all times.

I noticed that she began to dress and make herself up more naturally around Ben, less make-up, even a t-shirt and jeans occasionally. Monika's girl acolytes didn't bother to hide their displeasure at her transformation into a more casual person and lover of Ben Morrissey, but I didn't see it, as they did, as a betrayal of the character she had created. Instead, it seemed to me that she became so much more beautiful and more relaxed and so much more her true self in his presence.

One day Ben buzzed my apartment. He said that Monika had broken up with him. He said that he had never loved anyone like he loved her and that he would never love anyone again. He also said, vehemently, that she was a heartless bitch, and I don't know, maybe she could be, but if that was so, it was only in self-defense. I knew myself just how much Ben Morrissey could take you over body and soul. I was fine with that. Monika Lilac wasn't.

He said they were fighting about money. He wanted to know where her money came from, and she would never tell him. Ben thought that she had a wealthy lover or maybe several wealthy lovers who were keeping her afloat, enough so that she could afford champagne and grapes for breakfast and then nothing else all day until a steak for dinner at night, and of course all the films she needed to see and re-see. He said that she used sex as a weapon and that if she was displeased or wanted something sex would be withheld. And he also said that she never truly let herself go with him sexually. Always there was something she held back, and it was driving him crazy! Nuts! Fuck!

I tried to calm him down, but only half-heartedly. I felt that Ben was enjoying this situation, which was an unusual one for him. He got everything he wanted, always, and I think he was a little tired of that. Monika was older and difficult and a challenge, and so beautiful when she was beautiful that she put all of his other girls in the shade.

The phone rang and I picked it up. It was Monika so I gave Ben the phone and scurried to my bedroom, but I kept the door open to listen. Ben wanted me to hear everything and know everything about him, and if that isn't love, I don't know what is.

The Ben I heard on the phone was almost totally unbalanced by unrequited desire and jealous anger. He shouted at Monika and called her names, and I could only feel her impenetrable composure on the other end of the line. Finally, Ben started to cry, but he was still getting nowhere. He talked on and on in a quieter voice, and he begged her to see him, to sleep with him. She turned him down again and again, and she hung up on him. Ben hurled my phone across the room, and now he was really crying.

I cautiously re-entered the bright living room from my darkened little bedroom. Ben was sprawled out on the futon near the exposed red brick, spent. Then he started to laugh, and I laughed with him. He looked up at me and beckoned me over with those long fingers of his. "C'mere, you... what should we do tonight?" he asked as I settled onto the futon with him and submitted to being hugged and tickled.

"Should we see a movie?" I asked.

"NO!" Ben shouted, like a football coach. "No movies tonight." He asked me who I was seeing, and I told him about my doughboys again. He smiled widely and wanted to hear every last filthy detail for the umpteenth time. "Fuck, I'm so horny!" he said, jumping up off the bed and grabbing the phone back up off the floor and dialing any number he could think of for some girly company. He also wanted some cocaine. He called Tanya, who refused to come over and didn't have any drugs. Then he called some of the druggier girls from his circle, and a couple of guys. He laughed a lot but it was clear that he was getting nowhere.

He put the phone down and exhaled comically, blowing his lips out into a long raspberry. "Hey sweetie-pie, what do you know about this guy Murnau?" he asked. I told Ben that F. W. Murnau directed *Nosferatu,* the first real vampire movie, and *Sunrise,* which I said was one of the most beautiful films ever made.

"Wait, do you have *Sunrise*?" Ben asked, and I said I thought I did. I looked through some of the videotapes my parents had sent me from home and found my Foothill Video copy of *Sunrise*. "Can we watch it? Monika always talks about it," Ben said.

I said sure, and I turned out the lights and put the tape in and we lay back on the futon and watched it together. "Wow, that Woman from the City chick looks a lot like Monika!" Ben said, and it was true, she did. He was against the Woman from the City, played by Margaret Livingston, and the way she was breaking up the home of the Man (hunky George O'Brien) and his Wife (Janet Gaynor, with a Germanic braid on her head). But I felt sympathy for her, and by extension for Monika. The Woman from the City wanted excitement, and she wanted to take this sexy, muscular man back with her to the city as a prize.

"Wow, man," Ben said, when *Sunrise* was over. "I love Monika so much I don't know what to do." We lay there in the dark in silence for a little bit. "Do you think *you* can score me some coke, sweetie-pie?" he asked.

I had no idea how I would go about that, but I promised I'd try. I got up and put my tightest jeans on and my tightest t-shirt and leather jacket and my Sex Hat and went over to Rawhide to see what I might scare up. It was packed, luckily enough, and there were at least four likely middle-aged men with hungry eyes. I just had to pick one and hope he was the right one, so I held myself aloof in a "don't approach" way for about ten minutes while I figured out who was the best mark.

I finally settled on a really nasty/dirty looking bearded guy who kept tipping the go-go dancer on the makeshift platform in the middle of the bar. I positioned myself strategically in front of my mark for a time, shifting my weight appropriately. Finally I approached him, and I was very direct verbally and he was very direct physically and had his hand down the back of my pants pretty much instantly. I asked about coke. He cocked an eyebrow and said, "I'll see what I can do." I went to the restroom with him, and it was very quid pro quo, and I left Rawhide smiling.

I went back to the apartment feeling all refreshed and appreciated, innocent yet experienced, fresh yet soiled. Ben did the coke, and he started to tell stories he had told me many times before, but with that cocaine sense of having just discovered something really exciting. We were up til dawn and beyond. We went to sleep around noon.

On New Years 1999, Ben took me out to a male friend's house in New Jersey, and I spent the evening swinging on a tire swing in the backyard and drinking an entire bottle of cinnamon Schnapps. Yuck! I fell asleep on the grass, and I woke up the next morning to a dog licking my face, a slobbery

DAN CALLAHAN

friendly ugly dog, needy and insistent. Lord was it cold. I started shivering and my teeth started chattering as I scurried into the house, which looked like one big empty pizza box.

Boys and girls were draped over couches, passed out. Some were in each other's arms. It was even colder inside than it was outside. I saw a heavyset boy and a heavyset girl out on the porch. He was bending her over the railing and began to lightly spank her. It turned me on.

Ben couldn't find Monika at this point. They had had another fight and she had moved out. I hadn't seen her myself for some time when I encountered Tanya at one of those DIY group shows in a loft on the Lower East Side. She wasn't friendly and was even outright rude at first, as if I represented only Ben Morrissey to her, but I was seven or eight glasses of wine into the evening, so it was easy not to care about that. I mentioned Monika, and Tanya's formerly resentful face lit up with interest.

"Oh! The vamp! You know her, do you?" she asked.

I asked what she meant, and probably my face lit up with interest too, under the bleary drunkenness.

"I'm not into girls, but with her I was, you know?" she said. I told Tanya I understood exactly. She put a sharp-red-taloned hand on my shoulder and led me off into a corner of the gallery.

"She is a dream, she seduced me right away. I went to bed with her immediately without thinking, right?" she said. Tanya lit a cigarette. You could still smoke indoors then. "But she is crazy, all right? I'm not telling you something you don't already know, it's obvious, correct?" I nodded and started to get a little sober. "But listen, you do not know just *how* crazy this woman is. She has these, what do you call them, idée fixe?"

"Obsessions?" I offered.

"Yes, sure, obsessions, but mainly one, it's for a film of course, one of her *silent* films," she said, rolling her eyes derisively. "She is obsessed with finding the film of Murnau, the lost one, it's devils, how many devils? A couple of devils, a lost film, it's Murnau, you know him?"

I nodded, and Tanya got all affectionate suddenly, patting me under the chin. Maybe she had been drinking as much as I had, but we were on different courses, her up, me down. "Of course you do, sweetheart. You're one of those homosexuals who likes the ladies on the screen. I know you. You probably even like the ladies on the screen better than Ben Morrissey!" I blushed, because she was sort of right, but also because she had mentioned his full name. "You should go to bed with Monika, too," Tanya said, half-seriously. "It would do you good to sleep with a red-blooded lesbian, little boy."

It made sense to me, Monika and all her girls, but I hadn't thought of it before, that Monika was a lesbian. "But Ben and Monika are together now," I said, and Tanya snorted with laughter. "Of course! The two vamps! They will devour each other, it should be such fun to watch, we sell tickets! Me, I thought Monika only slept with men for money. That's what I thought, but what do I know?"

Tanya puffed at her cigarette furiously. "You are a gossipy little homosexual boy and you will probably tell this all over town, but I don't care, I *hate* Monika, and I don't care who knows it. You like to listen, right?" She had switched gears again, and I broke out in a sweat at the tone of her voice. "You watch, you listen, what else do you do?" she asked, like some Soviet interrogator. I told her about my middle-aged men. "Oh! Of course!" Tanya said. She threw her head back and laughed in a way that was eerily like Monika.

"This Manhattan, you sleep with people, you suck this and that but never for love!" she said, and then she looked at me with some compassion. "You love this Ben, right," she said, and it wasn't a question. I stood still, frozen. "You are his little boy slave, it is nice to have one." She took my face in her hands and stared at me unblinkingly. "Look, sweetheart, I don't give advice, I usually don't give advice, OK? But I give you some advice and you listen, get away from him. Leave, go somewhere else for a little bit. You're maybe nice, right? You are too nice. Get away for a little bit. Do it one more time and do it smart, get some money, and leave, go to Europe by yourself. Be by yourself for a little, leave the vamps here." She kissed me on the mouth, lingeringly, and we started to make out really, really ferociously in the far right corner of the loft. Tanya was the best kisser! I must have kissed her for an hour.

At some point she disengaged. I was all alone and I thought over what she had said. I looked in a mirror in the bathroom at the gallery and saw that I had Tanya's make-up smeared all over my face, and my my, I did look fetching in it. So I went up to G bar with all the make-up like that on my face, and I scored a four-way almost instantly with some hot guys in their thirties. The luck of the draw. It was a magic night, but I was thinking mainly about Tanya, who had revved me up, and Monika and Ben, too, while these three guys did expert licking, squeezing things to my body.

I wanted to see Monika, and Ben frantically wanted to see her, but he didn't know where she was staying. Monika rarely had an address to herself. She was one of these floating people who is always staying with someone, tip-toeing in, tip-toeing out, and she was so good at tip-toeing through those particular hospitality tulips that she never seemed to have to pay rent, or for food, or for anything most people need. What she did in return for certain men, I do not know.

I checked the repertory film listings in the *Village Voice* and scanned for anything that might be a likely Monika Lilac screening. The only one that looked like a Monika thing was Gloria Swanson in *Sadie Thompson* at the Museum of Modern Art. Monika didn't like Swanson, but she worshipped the film's director, Raoul Walsh, so I knew she'd probably be there.

I bought my ticket (I didn't have a membership then), and I stood in line with the same few elderly malcontents who went to everything at MoMa no matter what it was. They were fine with *Gone with the Wind* or the most minimalist experimental cinema because it was all the same to them. There was some melodrama when one of the old men accused another older man of cutting in line. "How *dare* you, how *dare* you!" he kept shouting, in the tone of someone confronting the murderer of their child. "HAVE YOU NO DECENCY?" he thundered. The older man hadn't even cut in line, as far as I could see, and what possible difference could it make? There were fifteen people waiting, tops. But that's the crowd at the Museum of Modern Art. Who knows what pressures and tribulations make these poor people what they are?

When we finally got inside, I sat close to the back so that I could keep an eye out for Monika. Time ticked, and the bearded, anal-retentive ticket taker, who looked just like the film director Mike Leigh, scanned the rows for any perceived misbehavior. Right before the lights went down, I noticed Monika, sitting in her spot. I'm not the most alert person, but I was there specifically to spot her, and there's no way she had come in through the door with the rest of us.

Did Monika have some kind of secret doorway she used? She just materialized in her seat, as far as I could see, and the lights went down, and we watched the movie, which was very good, but the ending was lost, alas, so a fine film concluded with a series of stills suggesting what the ending might have been like. I usually like suggestions over actuality, but not in this case. The missing reel at the end mutilated the movie.

The lights went up, and Monika had that force field around her as usual as she gathered up all her things. I approached her carefully, and when I tapped her on the shoulder, she turned around and looked at me sweetly, as if she'd expected to see me. "Oh Robert, wasn't Raoul gorgeous! He lost one eye and that ended his acting career, alas."

Yes, she said "alas," that was a Monika word, just as Ben's word was "whatever." We chatted a little bit. As we walked up the aisle, some of the black netting cape thing she was wearing brushed an older man on the head, and he started yelling at her, much too violently, but Monika just smiled fixedly and glanced back at him for a moment as if his outburst was a delightful two-reel comedy short. In fact, she leaned in to me and said, "He's very Mack Swain!"

Monika was at her most arch and self-conscious. She opened her mouth and let out a stream of talk that might have been pure gibberish or might have been something else, but there were Easter eggs of meaning hidden in the gibberish, so I tried to keep up, though I felt like I needed a translator. We went to La Bonne Soupe, a noisy French restaurant on 55th Street, and had some quiche and salad and heavy red wine.

She kept talking, great shooting streams of low talk, and I began to understand that she was on some quest to find a film called 4 Devils, the lost movie that F.W. Murnau made after Sunrise. "Let's just say I have a lead," she kept saying, crinkling up her face and wrinkling her nose coyly. This was a new mode she was in, a new persona she was trying, a kind of Myrna Loy coolness, and it didn't particularly suit her, but I always wanted to believe in Monika's various impostures, so I gave her all the imaginative attention I could as an audience member.

Then she stopped short, and she tried on another persona, with commanding quickness, a wary gun moll thing as she clasped my hand across the table and asked, "How is he?" I said he wasn't doing very well. Ben had stopped taking photos. He didn't eat much. He just lay around all day and smoked pot, and at night he snorted cocaine. Sometimes he cried. I spent a lot of time cradling Ben while he cried, and his crying gave me a huge erection that I had to do my best to hide and ignore while I cradled him. The big lug.

I didn't tell Monika all of this, but I made her know that he was unhappy, and I did mention the crying. She drew herself up and slowly nodded her head. "That's right, that's just what he needs," she said. "It will make him more human. It might make him nicer." Suddenly, Monika seemed super-smart, an expert puller of strings. I think she was smart, at times, but she hid it with all her dizzy affectations. She had brief illuminations, brief times when she spoke with a modicum of common sense, and these brief moments were always more impressive to me than any of her more outré exertions as den mother, cinephile femme fatale, and party girl.

She looked at me hard for a moment, skeptically. "What are we going to do with you, huh?" Now she was a Jewish mother, all warm and fuzzy and overwhelming. It was like she was playing hopscotch on any number of fragments of tried and quickly discarded personalities, and she had to keep moving as fast as she could before one of them stuck for good.

DAN CALLAHAN

"Who can I introduce you to?" she asked. "It's who you know in Manhattan, sweetie-pie, and don't ever forget that." That "sweetie-pie" really gave me the creeps, because she had obviously taken what she wanted from Ben Morrissey's personality and now she was using it on me. She might almost have become Ben for a few brief flashes, or a feminine version of him. I realized that I was very drunk. I had had almost all of two bottles of paint-thinner-like red wine while Monika hadn't had more than a few sips.

"Can I confide in you?" she asked, and I nodded vigorously, totally with her in that alcohol wavelength-strengthening way. "I'm worried about money. I know you can't do anything to help me, darling, but I just want to get this off my chest. I'm always worried about money, I need money for everything. I'm an extravagant person, you can see that, and I need a certain amount of money to make all this happen, alas. I get money from various places and various foundations. A lady always needs two bars and two foundations, that's one thing Louise Brooks said that I heartily concur with. That I heartily concur ..." her voice trailed off, and she stared away from me, into the distance.

We were enveloped in the noise of all the other conversations and the clattering silverware and the slurped soup and the whoops of conversational engagement around us, but we were both totally silent inside ourselves. That's Manhattan, too. You need all that outward clamor and dirt and uproar so that you can create the most impenetrable world of your own within it, a world of silence, of dreams stolen or created or half-created or fulfilled. Like when I touched The Scar on Ben Morrissey's Face.

We left La Bonne Soupe (I paid), and it was dark, winter, the wind was unforgiving. "Let's go see him," she said, and she raised her long arm to hail a taxi, her black batwing cape with the netting making a dramatic visual impression. She sat in the front seat of the cab when we got one, and we zoomed down to Chelsea where we found Ben in my apartment curled up on the futon, staring into space. "We're here!" Monika said, throwing her arms up so that she was a glamour bat entering the space, Irma Vep maybe, and Ben bolted right up and put his arms around her tightly and said, "Please forgive me, baby, just stay with me, please, don't ever leave me!" in a muffled, *very* intense voice.

They just stayed like that, hugging, unmoving, for a bit. They looked like brother and sister, with those dark curls of theirs. "I think we should watch a film. What do you have?" Monika asked, turning to me, with Ben's head still on her shoulder.

I didn't have too much to watch right then. Most of my videotapes were still at home, under the crawlspace in my parent's house. But I did have *Bringing Up Baby*, and so we watched that and *Stage Door* right after it, and we drank a good deal. Then we rewound the tape and started watching them again. It was a perfect evening. Ben said very little. Monika seemed happy, secure. There was nothing sexual in the air, no tension that I could discern. We just huddled together, fairly closely, and watched these two movies over and over again and drank and fell asleep sometime mid-day the next day. I left them on the futon and went into the bedroom to sleep, shutting the door, the iron door, on this couple I loved.

Something had altered for Ben and Monika. Maybe it was because she was clearly the one in charge now, but in any event, they became a couple that lots of people admired and envied, for a time. She went to his group shows, and gave him extensive feedback on his work, and she even took a few photos of him. Lots of people, critics and art enthusiasts, don't like the photos Monika took of Ben, but oh, I think they're just … well, in these photos, Ben has a look of total vulnerability, and I think this makes him more beautiful. Monika did, too, but his druggie friends and some of his art world patrons were unhappy. They viewed Monika as a kind of Yoko Ono, infantilizing their rugged macho photographer. Maybe they had a point, but if they did, it was a weak one. She just brought out a different side of him, that's all. And I think that softer side was more attractive, myself.

Arthur was particularly scathing about Monika when I bumped into him at one of Tanya's group shows. He practically spit in his fury at her. He had known her before in the late 1980s, and I wondered, not for the first time, just how old Monika was. "Do you know how old Monika is?" I asked Arthur, and he said, "Miss Channing is ageless, spoken like a press agent." He got drunk, and at a certain point he found me again, grabbed my hand, and said, "C'mon."

He pulled me into a taxi and put his hand down my pants in the backseat as if he still owned my body. He brought me up to his apartment, roughly pulled my clothes off, and had me again, on my back. Wordlessly, even soundlessly. It didn't hurt this time, because I was becoming more experienced. It was completely impersonal. When he was done, Arthur just said, "Get out." Arthur was an interesting guy.

I was getting freelance writing work, and that's when I interviewed Jeanne Moreau. She was getting a prize of some sort, and was flown in by the French Embassy or something. I had interviewed some actors and playwrights and such at this point, but I loved Moreau because I felt that she made being interviewed part of her art. We talked about Orson Welles, François Truffaut, Joseph Losey, Antonioni, but then we rushed right to the important things: Love, Death, Love again. Oh, she loved talking about love.

I sat there practically at her feet in her suite in The Pierre hotel. I drank champagne. She didn't. "I don't drink anymore," she said. I asked her why, and she shrugged. "I had just had enough of it, that's all." I learned more listening to Moreau all afternoon than I ever learned in college. I thought then that parents should just send their children to Jeanne Moreau for a day instead of sending them to college. Just give her the money. And then the kids could put on their résumé afterward, "Bachelor's degree, Moreau afternoon."

I took Monika to see some of Moreau's films, which had been programmed at the French Institute on 59th Street. La Lilac was particularly taken with *Moderato Cantabile*, a Marguerite Duras adaptation. That's a rare film, I haven't seen it in years, but I can still remember the way Moreau's character got drunk at a dinner party and went upstairs and took off her jewels as if they held the weight of the world.

I had kept the phone number of Moreau's assistant. I took a chance and called and asked if I might bring a friend up to meet the legend. The assistant said, no, no, no, no, Madame Moreau doesn't have a moment to spare. But the following day, when I went to meet Monika for lunch, there she was sitting with Moreau, who greeted me with that transformative smile of hers, the one that François Truffaut freezes for us in *Jules and Jim*. That was Monika Lilac for you. Magic! She got things done. I don't remember what we talked about. It might even have been a strained conversation, but Monika had made it happen, and she related to Moreau not as a fan but as an equal of sorts. No small feat.

It was summer again. I spent a lot of time shirtless on my roof getting a tan, calling phone lines to hook up with guys, sometimes two or three a day. Just getting a look and feel. A lot of the guys were older, overweight, weird-looking, and usually they were happy to see me in my shorts when I met them on the corner of 20th Street and Eighth Avenue, in front of a restaurant called Tazza, where I never ate once, but how many times did I say over the phone, "I'll be in front of a restaurant called Tazza, T-A-Z-Z-A, in tight shorts and flip flops."

Ben's career had flatlined for a bit. He wasn't moving forward, he was just staying in one place, and he couldn't get the solo show he wanted. He was tired of being the star of group shows, and he couldn't quite break out of them. We would hang out and drink to excess and he would take shots of me, but they weren't as good as they had been. He was getting sexier, though, to me at least, because he finally seemed a little insecure, or human.

He would let me hug him for a long time as we watched movies, and I told him about the guys I was seeing and he told me about Monika and how she had changed his life, and how she was magic. I agreed with him, she was magic. But I was a little worried about what might be behind this magic.

So yes, I was calling the phone lines a lot to hook up, and my money was still there in the bank, though it had dwindled a bit. Freelance writing work was only sporadic. I was going out all night drinking, and not just on Friday and Saturday, like most people. I'd be throwing back hard liquor on Tuesday at 6 AM. Fun! (And sometimes, Fun?) Ben was sometimes with me and sometimes not.

I'd go to screenings with Monika all during the summer and fall of 2000, and I fell more and more in love with her, and her magic, shall we say. I got to know her girls. I do think that Monika was basically lesbian, but I wouldn't be able to swear that she ever had any sexual contact with most of her girls. Then again, I wouldn't be able to swear that about guys either, except for Ben, and he admitted that they rarely slept together anymore, but that he loved and needed her more than ever.

Monika was above the sexual, maybe. Or that's what she wanted you to think. Tanya had told me otherwise, and what she said had been believable, but I think the bedding down with Tanya had come during an earlier period. Monika was a tactile person. She was always touching, caressing, embracing. And she talked about moviegoing in terms of "making love" to her eyes. "They are predatory, you know, dear, my eyes," she said to me once, staring right through me until I laughed. And embraced her. Monika. She made eye contact with me now because she seemed to trust me.

I kept having ever-rougher encounters with Arthur. He would see me at an opening, he would drink himself into a stupor, and always he would grab my hand and pull me in a taxi and have his way with me at his solo apartment in upper Chelsea and say, "Get out," or get in a shower afterward so that he wouldn't have to say it. It really was a peculiar thing. He really did act like I had no choice in the matter. He would smack me in the face and choke me, but it all seemed impersonal.

It was like he wanted to destroy me, but he couldn't. He was like somebody banging their head over and over again on a brick wall. Exposed brick! Very Chelsea. I guess deep down I felt he desired me on an extremely deep level, and he didn't know why, and it tormented him. His wounded fury really turned me on, and it also touched me. Something had twisted him into pretzel knots, and there was no way of untying them without his whole persona breaking. He used sex with me to release some of his anger.

I told Ben about this ongoing thing, and he was weirded-out at first,

DAN CALLAHAN

even mad at me, but then he just let it lie. Suddenly he had his first solo show, on the Lower East Side, in the winter of 2001. I don't know if my … I was going to say my "sleeping" with Arthur, but we never slept! Well, my "thing" with Arthur might have had something to do with that. Again, we come to, "Why not?" Or, let's face it, the more Muriel Spark-like, "Nevertheless."

There's a time for "Why not?" and there's a time for "Nevertheless." At the time, I felt, "Why not?" Years later, I mainly feel, "Nevertheless." Still, Ben was resplendent, if a touch too thin, in his blue agnès b. suit, with all his friends and acquaintances around him at the show, his show, his first solo show. And the photos of me had pride of place. The place itself was filled with mainly straight guys and girls, and so my photos were neglected or, worse, condescended to.

Ben had made me get an email address, finally, and I was working part-time doing editorial work at a newspaper where one of the computers had Internet access. Some of the older writers would bring in typewritten pieces to be scanned, and the younger ones often came by with floppy discs of their articles, so this was a clusterfuck period of technological transition.

Reviewing what passed for theater downtown, I saw some very ill-advised things. I righteously panned a play about Sylvia Plath in which Ted Hughes put on a Hitler mustache and *pushed* her into the oven, and I panned a musical about Princess Diana called *The Queen of Hearts*. In the first scene, amid trails of dry ice, Princess Grace descended from the rafters to lead poor Diana to heaven, and it only got worse from there.

I was getting lots of invites to random parties now and becoming something of an open bar professional. I liked staggering around the city drunk, up Sixth Avenue, down Eighth Avenue. Manhattan doesn't notice how drunk you are. Manhattan's cops might notice, though.

I was arrested and detained briefly around this time, for ducking under a PATH turnstile to New Jersey with Ben. The cops put me in handcuffs and threatened me with the Rikers Island prison before I could prove I was a resident with a phone call they placed to a co-worker of mine. I didn't have a driver's license or photo ID. If I'd been black, I know they would have sent me to Rikers and I probably would still be there. You don't get to make young mistakes when you're black in America. My consciousness was hardly raised about that fact then, but it is food for thought now for me to choke on.

The handcuffs came off and I went back with Ben to hang out in New Jersey in a spacious house with a bunch of writers, photographers, models, and actors who liked to get naked and swim in the pool. There was a lot of sex, but there were no gay guys, so I had beer and whiskey to keep me company, and this company was more than sufficient.

Arthur had given up trying to destroy me physically. Whenever I saw him now, he wore a sheepish and also slightly weaselly look. I could have done without it, but there was nowhere else for us to go with this combative thing we had, unless Arthur had wanted to actually murder me, maybe. He had to back off entirely.

We were at a show of Robert Mapplethorpe photos, portraits of downtown '80s stars, Blondie and so forth, not the S & M photos. Arthur came up behind me and slapped me hard on the back and said, "He would have liked *you*." I raised my eyebrows and said, "I doubt it." Arthur's face tightened even tighter. He was a lethally *sharpened* pencil. "Maybe you're right," he said, walking away.

I had moved out of my Chelsea one-bedroom and into a so-called "furnished room" off Second Avenue and 7th Street in the East Village that was little more than a hallway that ended in a window that looked out on the street. It was coffin-like, but the location and the price ($175 a week) were not to be ignored.

There was no kitchen, so I had to learn to eat out on a budget. How many tasteless slices of pizza have I had for dinner! And the goddamn pizza bagels from that Bagel "Café" on Third Avenue and St. Marks Place! I'd always need one of them ($1.50) when they had been sitting there for hours and they were cold and the cheese on the bagel was this gelatinous, faded gray thing on top of the depressed tomato sauce. I would go to a party and there would be the most extravagant piles of food and drink, little slices of filet mignon and slices of potato and sour cream and chive and caviar on top and dry champagne. And then the next day I would make do with those goddamn pizza bagels and a twenty-ounce 7-Up.

Money in Manhattan, or the lack of it. I made my rent every week from my newspaper job, copyediting and sometimes assigning work to writers old and new, fine and hopeless, neurotic and reasonable. But I didn't have any money left over to eat anything but those pizza bagels. Oh, and Sbarro on Broadway and 8th Street had a special where you could get spaghetti and meatballs and bread and a drink for $1.75, but only from 2-4 PM. I ate that a lot.

I was living close to Kim's Video then, the one on St. Marks off Third Avenue. I had looked around the Kim's Video off Washington Square Park when I was in college, and I had even briefly worked at the Kim's deep in the West Village on Bleecker Street in my last year of college.

There were still four or five Kim's Videos in operation in 2001, and they were run by the mysterious Mr. Kim, whom I never once saw. The Kim's on St. Marks was the largest of his outlets—it had three grungy floors. The first floor was for music, and you climbed the stairs with the walls plastered with stickers and random movie posters to the second floor, which sold videos and, later, DVDs. The top floor was all movie rentals, organized by country and director, from Robert Aldrich to Andrzej Żuławski. Paradise!

I got my film education at Kim's Video, with its mean hipster all-male staff, its eerie quiet, its ratty video boxes. I watched all of Fritz Lang's films first, in order. Kim's had bootlegs of films that hadn't been commercially released, so it was a completist heaven. I came in every day, pretty much, and the famously unfriendly clerks got so used to me that they would actually tell me about, say, a new widescreen copy of Nicholas Ray's *Bigger Than Life* that had just come in, or a new Frank Borzage, or a new King Vidor.

One rental was only $1.25 if you brought it back before 11 PM. Kim's Video always felt amiably gloomy and empty even when it was filled with people, like some abandoned warehouse in a dream, like a girl whose hair is going gray who nobody had ever wanted to dance with. It was a treasure chest. Sometimes I skipped the pizza bagel and went for the film. When I told Monika about this, she nodded approvingly, though she was one of those cinephile purists who only watched films in a theater if she could help it. "Sometimes I succumb," she would sigh, as though admitting to a crime because she had watched Colleen Moore in *Orchids and Ermine* on video in the living room of one of her girls.

I was at Kim's with Ben one night when I asked him about Monika's girls. My boyfriend Carlo Rossi and I had spent a lot of quality time together earlier in the evening, so I just came out with it: "Is she sleeping with them, with one of them, or all of them, or what?" I sputtered. "Do you watch, do you participate, how does this work?" I hadn't been looking at Ben, or looking up at him, ha ha, when I said this, and when I did, his black eyes were especially twinkly.

"Sweetie-pie," he said in his lowest voice, "let's not get too deeply into this, but let's just say that at this point I benefit from this relationship in pretty much every conceivable way, OK?" I laughed, snorted, actually, and bent down to look at the new Kim's bootlegs at the front. "You dork," Ben said, reaching down to shake me and smack my face playfully. "I bet you were one of those guys in high school who snorted milk out of his nose when you laughed, weren't you?"

I squirmed away from him and said, "You know me too well." There was a little bit of silence, as we pretended to look at video boxes. "I love you, sweetie-pie," Ben said in this really scary-wonderful intense voice. "I love you, too," I said. When I said it I felt like I was being burned alive for a split second, and I wanted to be burned alive all the time.

We went back to my hallway on 7th Street, and we sat down on my narrow, sagging bed, provided by the realty company that rented the so-called furnished rooms, and I slipped in a tape of a rare German silent movie starring Henny Porten, who had been idolized by a young Marlene Dietrich. Ben was fully on board with this cinephile way of life now. He wasn't a natural cinephile by nature, but it didn't take him long to develop an almost voracious enthusiasm for the most obscure Kim's tapes, the black plastic boxes marked with a yellow pen that contained the really far-out items, the forgotten films, the neglected, the odd, the films lost in shadows, decaying, spliced, hissing, popping, shaking, flickering, films lost under films, a maze, as maze-like as the social performance of the woman who called herself Monika Lilac.

We looked at the film, which wasn't all that good but was definitely watchable. We were sitting close together on the bed. Ben's solid left thigh was touching my much smaller right thigh. I could hear him breathing. The film was silent and had no musical accompaniment. The only sound was Ben's breathing and the human hoots and whoops and the car noises down in the street.

There were four bars on my block then. Everybody was drunk and shouting at all hours. I tried not to hear it, or to hear it just faintly, but the truth was that I was getting tired and run-down at this point. I felt like cars were running over my head every night, and the nights were so hot. It was only April, but it was ninety to a hundred degrees every day.

The film had ended, but the tape just kept playing. Ben kept up his steady breathing. I glanced at the rise and fall of his stomach. "Monika gives me everything I want," Ben said, "and things I never knew I wanted. I love some of her girls, too. But she's the main love."

"The main love," I repeated. "And then you have … it's Bohemian, I guess. We believe in free love. We learned about *free love* in Greenwich Village," I whispered. Ben laughed, and I did, too.

"I wish you didn't have a cock," Ben said. "I wish you had tits. I wish I could get hard for you, but I can't. I don't think I can. Is that all right?" He laughed, and it was a very sad laugh.

"That's all right," I said.

"You've given me so much, and … I don't know," he said. He pulled me over and got on top of me and put his mouth on mine. His tongue went in my mouth. He started to dry hump me a little. But he wasn't hard. Finally he stopped. "Fuck," he said. "You're so bristly."

I started to cry. Those goddamn drunks outside, those street noises, they filled all the space around us when I wanted so much for there to be total silence. And we were so unbecomingly sweaty from the heat. "You know, buddy, a girl can do it and she doesn't have to be aroused, right?" he asked with a Californian upward inflection. I cried harder. "C'mere," he said. He licked the tears off my face. "What do you want from me?" he asked. "What would satisfy you? What can I give you?"

"Can you take your clothes off and let me kiss you all over?" I asked, quick as a shot. And quick as a shot right back, Ben took his shirt off and his pants off, and he stood up in his underwear and turned on the light by my TV. He was wearing tighty-whities. He had never looked more beautiful, more carnal, more a tall drink of water and tree trunk and icon.

"I'm going to do this seriously," he said. "Don't let me make a joke of this, don't let me get away with that." He slowly took his underwear down. This was the first time I really and truly saw Ben Morrissey naked. All of him, in the light, just standing there naked, all for me. It was better than I could have possibly imagined, and I'm quite an imaginer.

"How do you want me?" he asked in that quiet intense voice again.

"Could you just lie down on your back?" I asked. I was so scared I could barely breathe. But I was so thrilled I was barely scared.

Ben lay down, and his huge feet hung off my bed. He was too tall for it, he was too tall for everything. "I'm yours, sweetie-pie. I can't get hard, probably, but do whatever you want to me." A Christian martyr!

He didn't get hard, and I didn't try to make him hard. I was hard the whole time, almost two hours. For almost two hours, I had access to Ben Morrissey's body. I didn't take advantage of that. I was very gentle and as respectful as possible. I just kissed him a lot, everywhere. The bottoms of his feet, his knees, his stomach (he laughed), his neck (his breathing got very heavy), and yes, his balls and his dick sometimes. He got semi-hard at one point. We were very young. I asked him to get on his stomach. I kissed his back and the backs of his knees. I was tentative. He lifted his head and smiled at me. "Do whatever you want, sweetie-pie," he said in a very forceful tone of voice.

Like the crack of a whip or the slam of a door Ben finally got up and got on top of me and jerked me off until I came. Right before I came, he said, "I love you." I said, "I love you," right back, and we were staring right at each other. It was *extremely* intense. Ben Morrissey!

When we were done I giggled, and he laughed. We drank for a long time, lots of Carlo Rossi, and then another jug after I went out to the all-night liquor store and came back. We drained almost all of that jug, too. We were so close. We breathed together. Before we passed out, Ben slurred, "I want to watch you fuck a woman. You have to do that for me. I pick the woman, and I get to watch. Can you get hard for that?"

"If you're watching," I slurred right back, "I probably can. I'd need to be really drunk."

"That goes without saying, dude," Ben said. He was ultra-macho now, of course. "Everybody thinks we're doing it," he said, "so we might as well quasi do it sometimes since we have that reputation anyway. You know, maybe I can get hard for you if you wore a bra and some slutty little cotton panties for me and shaved your face really close and hid your dick away? It would have to be, like, a sleight of hand, or like, a trick of perspective? Let's sleep on it." It was daybreak. We slept through the day. We ignored it. We had won a victory, somehow, or so I felt at the time. Whatever. Alas. I don't look forward to my demise. Or maybe I do. I don't know.

I walked the streets at random then, and I would hear, "Sign the petition, animal rights!" Actually, it was, "Sign the pe-ti-tion! An-i-mal rights!" There was this harsh-faced, whip thin lady with cropped hair who was always on a corner of Astor Place or on Sixth Avenue and 8th Street in this period who would stand in front of a table displaying gruesome photos of kitty cats with their eyes missing or some such, and she would ceaselessly cry, "Sign the pe-ti-tion! An-i-mal rights!" Sometimes she would harass young couples who passed her table. This lady was very much part of the texture of those times in Manhattan. I disliked her intensely.

She was a classic New York crank, and I have no idea what "the petition" was or why we needed to see those nauseating kitty mutilation photos all the time as we walked down the street in the Village. I saw her make two girls cry, two separate girls on two separate occasions. But one day I passed her table as I was walking with Monika, and the lady put down her clipboard for a moment and just stared after Monika. It was a rare human moment for this lady. It was a moment of desire. It made me even more grateful to know Monika.

It was so hot that I couldn't sleep at night and I would sit out on the stoops across the street at 3 AM and drink lukewarm ginger ales and 7-Ups from a deli on Second Avenue, also a hallway. (The building it was in blew up due to an illegal tap into a gas main in 2015, and the explosion killed two people.) Nothing was cold, everything was hot and the heat rose off everything. Meryl Streep was playing Arkadina in Chekhov's *The Seagull* in Central Park, an Event then, and I went to review it. I was barely conscious in the heat from sleep deprivation and dehydration as Streep acted all over the place (she did a cartwheel at one point, that I remember). It was heat stroke time. We were riding for a fall, all of us.

August of 2001, Monika hosted another party. This party was a silent comedy party and it was held in Brooklyn, I can't remember where. I've lived in Brooklyn for years now, but I still get confused about various neighborhoods. It was given at a large warehouse space, and it seemed like it might actually have been a space where a film might have been made. It had a soundstage feel.

There were dueling projectors all over the place playing Charlie Chaplin and Buster Keaton movies. Monika had set it up so that it did seem like a competition between them, Charlie and Buster. Most of her girls were dressed as either Chaplin or Keaton. Before the party, to prepare me, maybe, Monika had told me an illuminating story.

Geraldine Chaplin, Charlie's daughter and a very fine actress, had brought home a boyfriend in the late 1960s. The boyfriend was all caught up in Buster Keaton screenings at his college, and he didn't care at all about Chaplin, and he told the great man himself that he liked Keaton better in a casual tone of voice. Chaplin was nonplussed, to say the least. Then deeply dismayed, silent for a few moments, just thinking this over. "But *I* am an artist!" he finally cried. Keaton was too, of course, and even more of one, or a better one, I think, because he was incapable of thinking of himself in such self-important terms.

Monika had engaged a pianist to play sprightly tunes of the 1920s at the front of the space. I'm more Buster than Charlie, so I was dressed as Buster Keaton in a porkpie hat, and Ben came as Max Linder, an elegant comedian of the '20s, now obscure, and he won points for this with Monika, who was wearing a blonde wig and a pastel, soft-looking dress, very attractive. I asked her, via inter-title, who she was supposed to be, and she widened her eyes, made her mouth into a little dot, and wrote down on her own inter-title, "Marion Davies."

She led me over to a projector that was playing Davies in *The Patsy*, and I stood there and watched all of it. I was completely entranced by Davies in that movie, especially when she does impressions of other silent stars toward the end. She did Pola Negri, Gloria Swanson, and Lillian Gish, and her takes on all three were hilariously detailed and accurate. Monika watched this scene with me, and she kept doubling up with laughter. Marion watching Marion.

The space was set up with "Pratfall Slides," where you could fall and slip to the end of the warehouse. Some of the girls were so delighted with this slide that they just kept sliding to the end of it and getting up and going back to slide again. There were tables with seltzer water bottles that could be used to spray whomever you liked, and the girls kept running round and round the space and kicking each other and making wide-eyed, open-mouthed faces.

I watched some of *The Gold Rush* with Charlie, then some of *College* with Buster, and I started to watch Davies in *The Patsy* again because I couldn't get enough of her. I sprayed Ben with some seltzer and I got sprayed back, and we chased Monika around and around the space and made goofy faces and slipped onto the Pratfall Slide, zoom!, all the way to the end and back again.

I broke away for a while and watched the pianist pounding away at his piano, "Ain't We Got Fun," and tunes like that. At a certain point I turned around and was confronted by not just one Buster Keaton but two Buster Keatons … my doughboys! We recognized each other, and we tried to stay in character for a few moments, but pretty soon we had retired to a dark corner of the space and we were three Buster Keatons making out, three stonefaces kissing under porkpie hats.

They were so tall and their hands felt so good on me. One of them started to shake me a little bit, for some reason, and I shook him back, and then we were all three shaking and kissing and groping, and they lifted me up again and threw me on the Pratfall Slide. They kept picking me back up at the end of it and putting me back on it.

We were laughing now, so that we were all dressed like Buster but we weren't really stonefaces anymore, and finally they carried me deeper into the building and found a huge deserted room and pulled my pants down and started doing terrifically dirty things to me. It was extremely intense. We made no sounds. I kept finding Paradise then.

VI

So yes, Paradise lost. I'm not going to go too deeply into that. I was here in the city. I hate reading about it. I hate when anybody writes about it. So let me suggest it quickly. The smell isn't really describable, and it lasted for months. There were several occasions on the street and on the subway when I heard viciously anti-Semitic free-floating hostilities. There was a man with a Jamaican accent who preached hellfire and just desserts on the subway who would follow you from car to car. Fear and paranoia and dismal fantasies of revenge soaked into everything.

I lost my job and couldn't find another one. My money dwindled. By the beginning of 2002, I was at the end of my tether. Jeanne Moreau called me. She still had my number. She asked if I was all right. I told her yes, yes, I was fine, but I wasn't. When even Jeanne Moreau is looking outside of her splendid self, you know that something is wrong. "If you come to France, I will cook for you," she offered. If I'd had any money, I would have gone, but when you have no money, you're stuck, and I was stuck in Doom City.

I was still living in my hallway in the East Village, going to Kim's Video every day. I didn't have money for food, but I always had money for a film rental. Ben was in Europe with his drug posse. He had gone there after the silent comedy party, and he hadn't returned after the disaster. I wondered if he'd ever come back. We hadn't even properly said goodbye. He sent me short letters and short emails and asked me to look after Monika, who was difficult to reach then even when you did reach her.

I love the wistfulness of a first name and a last name. That comes, perhaps, from being so marked by the television show *My So-Called Life* when I was in high school. Everybody said and used a first and last name on that show, for extra 1990s woebegone oomph. Angela Chase. Jordan Catalano. Rayanne Graff. Brian Krakow. Rickie Vasquez. All of those names are magic to me. What's in a name? A rose. I wonder what became of those people on that show. They'd be my age now, or just a little older. I doubt Angela wound up with either Jordan or Brian. They were in high school, after all. I have a feeling Rayanne isn't doing well. And that Angela doesn't talk to her anymore and has repeatedly ignored her Facebook friend requests.

Here's a name of mine: Heinz Laranthal.

We were halfway into 2002. My money was almost gone, and I couldn't hang on much longer. So I took a job. One of those times where you "take any job." It was a rude awakening. I was paid to pick up the phone in a real estate office. There were about twenty lines, and sometimes three or four of them would go off at once, and I would put them on hold, one, two, three, until I could send them out to the floor where the calls were sent to select agents. I drank an ice coffee every morning. It was from 9 AM to 6 PM, Monday through Friday. Worse than school, worse than anything.

I remember being on the subway during this period with two older ladies who looked like secretaries. Office workers. Beaten down, pretty miserable-looking, but good-humored. They were reading a paper that said Mariah Carey had been hospitalized for exhaustion. That's what the secretary on the left reported. She was smaller, birdlike. The secretary on the right was a bigger woman, Italian, probably, large eyes, heavily lined face, lots of make-up. She did a wised-up look and croaked, in a very thick Bronx accent, "I wish *I* could be hospitalized for ex-haw-tshun."

A notable choreographer I had met and slept with a few times sent me a discreet email invitation to his latest evening of dance, or rather his company did. I used to pretend with him that I was auditioning to get into his dance troupe—as a sexual role play scenario—and before we had sex he would actually teach me about dance and how I had to "use levels" and "dance against the rhythm of the music." He was working on dances set to Duke Ellington music then. Once he said, "You're just as good as anyone in my company." I don't think it was a particularly sincere compliment, but I liked hearing that, all the same.

I went by myself to the dance. I could have brought a guest, but I was feeling antisocial then, badly used, marking time. The evening was playing in a spanking new dance center in Chelsea. The seating was spacious, just rows leading up and up with all the room you needed, quite a relief for someone who had been reviewing Broadway shows at theaters that had been built in a time when people were as small-framed as Mary Pickford and Douglas Fairbanks. I was feeling a little sorry for myself. I remember sitting there in the half-light of the theater, staring into space. I watched the dance, and I noticed Heinz Laranthal in it, but not all at once, somehow.

In the lobby afterward the choreographer touched my shoulder. And then Heinz was rushing up to me, all thick shiny parted cute-boy hair with bangs and bitey even teeth bared in a smile, and he was grabbing me by the shoulders. "Who are you?" he asked, shaking my shoulders and running his hands down my arms. He had a Swiss-Austrian look, like he should be wearing lederhosen and a green peaked cap and drinking light beer and licking whipped cream, and his "well?" eyes were the lightest hazel and slightly filthy-crazy, and his mouth was thick and impudent.

His nose was slightly large for his face when he turned in profile, but this extra size, coupled with the thickness of his lower lip, made him very obviously sexy, as did the unexpected thicket of chest hair poking out of his black t-shirt. After he asked me who I was, he did a classic Heinz thing: he made his face a blank and cocked his head, like he was signaling you, "I'm *dumb* and sexy!" Even though the fact of him doing it, and it was a consistent mannerism, meant that he wasn't really dumb at all but could play it as a part for effect.

"I'm friends with him," I said, which wasn't quite true. Heinz's eyes got even wider and his mouth fell open, which was the next level of his "I'm dumb and sexy!" act, and pretty much irresistible, I thought.

"No!" he said. "He has no friends! I've been in his company for like two years and he never even says hello to me! Who *are* you?" he asked again. This time he moved closer to me and projected a powerfully direct kind of interest in me. I got hard right away. Heinz smiled again (those choppers of his!), and moved even closer and said, "I have to tell you something." I grimaced in my drunken way and said, "What?" and he leaned right next to my face and said, "You have an eyelash on your cheek." I asked which one, and he said, "Your left cheek."

I closed my eyes and brushed my left cheek. "Is it gone?" I asked, with my eyes still closed. "Yes, it's gone now," Heinz said. He stayed very close to my face and peered at me. He stared at me unblinkingly with those candid eyes. I lifted my right arm up and brushed his glossy bangs away from his forehead a bit. We were alone together.

Heinz put his arms around my shoulders and started to dance with me a little. Not Ben's box waltz, but a slow dance, a high school dance. We were almost the same height, but he was slightly shorter. He smelled good, surprisingly musky, a masculine smell, but with chocolate chip cookie dough mixed in. All that chest hair. He was a man and he was a boy. I was unsteady on my feet.

"How much have you had to drink?" he asked.

"Only drunks count their drinks," I said. "I heard that somewhere once."

"Is that true?" Heinz asked, pulling back and cocking his head, like he really wanted to know, like it was really important. "I should stop counting then, it's this profession, it's all counting, it's all numbers, music, you know? Do you have a favorite composer?"

"I like Brahms," I said.

Heinz's Mr. Potato Head mouth blurred into a warm grin. When he was sweet, you got the closed-mouth grin. The smile with the large teeth bared was for conquest. "Right." He leaned into me and rested his head on my shoulder and started grinding his hips into me. Not discreetly either. He was nuzzling my neck gently, but below the waist he was grinding into me. It took a little while, but the choreographer finally came up to us and said, "Behave yourselves," in a low, not unfriendly voice, and then he swept away.

Heinz pursed those thick red striated lips of his. "Like, *whatever,*" he said, and it wasn't Ben's "whatever," it was the "whatever" of an old-time Valley Girl. "You want to go to a party?" Heinz asked. "My friend is having a party, it's on this block ... but hey, wait, I need to catch up with you." Heinz grabbed and downed several champagne flutes in a row.

I was in love with Heinz already. "I'm in love with you already," I said. Alcohol, how about that?! You see, that's what alcohol is for. Heinz heard this and didn't react, really. He was stonefaced in a way that made me worry, and this worry only increased my love, or my infatuation. Maybe he knew that?

"Don't be too serious yet," he said.

"OK," I said.

"I mean, we can be serious later on tonight, when we're having *sex,* you can be as serious as you want, and I'll be serious, too. Or I'll like try to be. Let's get out of here."

We left and went out into the night and it was cold and I started to shiver. Heinz had on a bulky heavy fur-collared coat. "Hey, you're shivering." He opened the coat and came at me very aggressively and backed me into one of those closed silver awnings and wrapped me in the coat and opened his mouth and kissed me.

When he kissed me, it was like breaking through the surface of water and getting air after holding your breath for so long that you thought you might die of suffocation. His mouth was open and my mouth was open and we didn't "kiss" like people do in movies or in their bedrooms or wherever. No. It was just that Heinz had opened up his mouth and taken me in and we just stayed like that. Of course! Just stay like that. Don't peck and smooch and do all that other nonsense.

So my mouth was open on his mouth, and this was kind of a smile, for both of us, and yes, he got his tongue in my mouth, but he did detailed, unusual things, like running his tongue against the top of my front teeth and the back of them. So specific. He made these hot little "umm, umm" sounds and put his hands on the back of my head. I did the same with him, and I applied extremely forceful pressure on the back of his head, the sort of pressure that meant, "You're not going *anywhere*," and I could feel him accept this and almost laugh a bit, or laugh as much as he could as his mouth (it was such a large mouth) tried to cover the whole lower half of my face.

He was a smoker. I loved his slightly sour smoker's breath. We both got a little giggly for a time, through our noses, but then we just got deeper and deeper into it, making underwater sounds and holding our heads tightly in place with our hands ... he had started to apply extremely forceful pressure of his own to my head. Oh God, please, just to stay like this. Can't we stop now? It's so quiet here now.

I think we were like that against the silver awning for ... a half hour? Forty-five minutes? A month? A year? Always? I hope so. Life went on around us. We were in Chelsea, so we didn't have to worry too much. We got a few wolf whistles. Two separate people, a guy and a girl, shouted, "Get a room!" at us. It wasn't overly sexual, our Kiss. I don't know. I wasn't there. I was inside of it, not outside of it.

Heinz Laranthal just had me up against an awning with his textured, fur-collared, almond-colored coat wrapped around me and his thick, insistent lips open on mine. He went "umm" and "umm" quietly. Our hands went further down sometimes, and he rubbed my crotch once or twice, but carefully, like an afterthought, or like, we'll have time for this later. We have all the time in the world.

To break the spell, Heinz knew he had to be rough. The Kiss was broken by him and he looked at me wildly, with hard, candid, "what the fuck?" eyes. He slammed me back harder against the awning and rammed his tongue into my right ear. It would have been a momentary action for most people, but Heinz went the full distance with it. He used his tongue in my right ear to attack me, in a way, and as he kept jutting it into my ear further and further and harder and harder he forced my arms up over my head on the awning and held them there. He didn't look strong, but he was—he had walked on his hands momentarily in the second dance piece. That image came back to me as he pretty much sexually assailed my ear on the street against the awning with his tongue. It sounds silly, but it wasn't at all silly when you were inside of the space that he created with you.

He stopped and looked at me again. "Should I let you go?" he asked. I "squirmed" for him, I "struggled" against him. "So who are you, exactly?" he asked. "You gonna let me find out, *huh*?" That "dumb" Valley Girl inflection again, the cocked head, the "blank" face. I was the best kind of drunk right then. It was like being up, up, up really high somewhere where no one can get at you, on some paper-thin ledge, and I wasn't scared of falling because that kind of fear had been eradicated.

He let me go and said, "Put your hand in my mouth." I put my right hand in his mouth. He did this all-out animal-like movement with his head, bobbing it back and forth against the rhythm of what most humans might have fallen into, sucking hard on each of my fingers like some vacuum-cleaner gone berserk, sucking up all the dust and dirt and making everything clean. Chocolate chip cookies for everyone!

He took my hand out of his mouth and put it on his face. "What do you want, huh? *Huh?*" He looked like he might punch me or bite me. I was breathing heavily and I was starting to get overwhelmed and I felt like I was going to cry, and I held the tears in, but he could see what I was doing. There was no hiding from him. "Oh, you're a sensitive boy, huh?" he said. It wasn't really a question, but most of what he said sounded like a challenging quasi-question. Heinz was an upward inflection.

"You can cry a little, nothing scares me," he said. Two tears rolled silently down my face. Of course he licked them. Ben had done that once. But Ben kept me at a distance. His love for me was a shut door. Everything about Heinz was come inside, wrap my coat around you, but he wasn't a warm cup of cocoa, or if he was, you felt that there might be a switchblade next to it, not that he would cut you, but he might just like the sound it made when it opened. This is just movie knowledge, I've never heard a switchblade open in life, have you? In a movie, I know exactly the sound effect usually used when a switchblade opens. Open up. Why not?

Heinz got all rough again, putting his mouth on my mouth, and we fell naturally down onto the sidewalk. We were not on a deserted street by any means (it was 19th Street between Seventh and Eighth Avenue), so we heard plenty of catcalls and plenty of "Get a room!" Rooms were for later. What we were doing now had to be done on the street, in the cold, against an awning, on the sidewalk. I could have *lived* just down there with Heinz on the sidewalk with his mouth on mine and in fact I did. It's funny how all that time passes so tediously at school or a job you don't like, but then with Heinz on 19th Street that night every few seconds was filled with some illumination and some revelation of pleasure.

He took his mouth off mine and playfully held my arms back over my head again, this time on the sidewalk. He said, "You're, like, romantic, right? Or you have romantic tendencies, right?" I closed my eyes and my head shied to the left when I said, "Yeah." He laughed and pulled my head back up and said, "Open your eyes, look at me!" I happily did as I was told. "OK, I find this shyness of yours *way* too charming," Heinz said, and we both giggled like the schoolgirls we were. Masculine, feminine, a film by Godard, 2003, on the streets of Chelsea. A film found on a sidewalk.

"What am I going to do with you, huh?" he asked, and I said, "Everything," right away. I was completely unguarded, and so was he because he said, "You might not like everything." I said, "I'll *like* not liking the things I don't like about everything," and he said, "Fuck! You're a pervert, too!" I shouted, "YEAH!" He pulled my shirt up out of my pants and started just unrestrainedly licking my chest, and this was deeply hot and deeply unfair. I felt like I might pass out from too much pleasure. Too much pleasure, a memoir of a woman of the streets!

"Please, please, stop!" I said, and it was sort of a genuine plea. He mumbled, "You don't want me to stop," and kept doing it. I repeated back, "I don't want you to stop." Back and forth. "You don't want me to ever stop," he said, and I said, "I don't want you to ever stop," and he said, "I'll never stop," and I said, "You'll never stop."

Heinz licked very slowly now at the top of the waistband of my black Banana Republic underwear, and he stopped. It was a full stop, a decisive stop. He put his right hand in my mouth, and I didn't want to compete with what he had done with me so I just let his fingers explore in there. "I wonder what would excite you most," he purred. It was a purr, it was feminine. "Should I just like *blow* you right here on the street? Would that excite you?" He laughed, and he sat down on me and started to grind back and forth and did his "I'm dumb and sexy!" face. It was even hotter and funnier the second time. "You look so helpless, it's so cute," he said.

Something surged in me and I got up and grabbed his face with both my hands and started to make out with him as violently as I possibly could. Very different from our first unmoving kiss, with those distant "umm" sounds of his. I was basically replicating the intensity of that legato kiss but making it all staccato and jabby and chewy and bitey. Of course he rose right up to the level I was at, and he kept trying to match it, but I kept dominating him and grabbing his body in the dirtiest, pinchiest ways I could think up on the fly. Sometimes he would let out a shout of surprise, a very masculine yelp. Fuck. There is nothing hotter than the sexual power struggle between two versatile gay boys.

We were struggling on the sidewalk but slowly inching up the awning, so that we were on our knees, and Heinz started to get the better of me. He held my face in his hands finally and kept my head still, in a vice, really, so that he could just look at me. His face was very different now. His chin was down, and he was staring up at me with his mouth slightly open and his brown eyes staring right into me.

"I'm going to bite you," he said in a really low voice. His face softened a little when he said, "It feels like the thing to do," in the tone of voice of a doctor or nurse in a hospital comforting a patient. "Where are you going to bite me?" I asked. My voice sounded to me like a frightened little kid who's excited by his own fear. "I don't know yet, stay with me," Heinz said. And I said, "I'll stay with you, I'll stay."

The energy changed again. I heard the sound of heavy female boots clunk clunking on the sidewalk, and geysers of echoing feminine laughter shooting up into the night. "What are we going to do?" Heinz asked, and I answered, "Everything." He laughed a little, and his laugh sounded genuinely scared.

"OK, I will bite you, at some point, later, OK? Right now I'm just going to give you the nastiest fucking hickey on your neck that you have ever had in your whole fucking life—" and he had attached himself to the right side of my neck and forced me back down to the ground before he had finished talking. And he wasn't kidding. I'm very ticklish and sensitive pretty much everywhere on my body, so this all-out assault on what just about anyone feels is a vulnerable area really sent me into a tailspin of pain/pleasure/fear/pain/pleasure all the way down to the earth then crash then fire all over the plain.

The drunkenness was coming in waves now and reinforcing and maybe even creating some of our interactions. I passed out of what had been an in-between vague drunkenness back into full-out, exultant, I love all of you! drunkenness. That is not a level of euphoria that's available to human beings without some kind of chemical alteration, notwithstanding the various forms of meditation, notwithstanding the bangarang lyric improvisational carnality of Heinz Laranthal. An epoch later, or an eternity of twenty minutes where again I felt more than I had in whole years of my life, he was looking down at me and grinning a queeny drunk grin that closed his eyes slightly, just slightly, and saying, "We should go to this party."

I said right away, "No! Please! Can't we stay here like this?" He laughed and asked, "Like, *forever*?" I said yes. He looked down on me, loomed over me and said, "OK. We can't, like, in actuality, but we've found a groove." I said, "I might never find it again," and he said, "Right, so you're really, like, *romantic*, right?" I closed my eyes. "Wow, you're really something," he said. "You're something else." I said, "So are you," with my eyes still closed, and I opened them to look at Heinz. I couldn't read his face.

He put his hand on my crotch and kept squeezing it. "So, is, like, horniness at the base of all this romanticism, is that what it is?" he asked. I whispered, "*No*, not at all, for me," and he said, "You're so dramatic." I said, "Do you find that attractive?" but it wasn't a question. "Do you like Ravel?" he asked. I said I only knew *Bolero* and that I thought it was silly. "No! No! No! Bad boy!" he said, very queeny, smacking my face. "You're Brahms and I'm Ravel, so, like, you need some Ravel, and maybe I need some Brahms. Is that what this is?" he asked. It wasn't a question.

"I have a crummy job. Should I just quit?" I asked. "I have to pick up a phone and it drives me nuts." I had been picking up that twenty-lined phone for three months. "Yes. If you're even asking that question, the answer is yes," he said, lighting up a cigarette.

"How long have you been a smoker?" I asked.

"Since I was, like, ten," Heinz said. "So ... we're just gonna stay here, huh?" he said. "We're gonna live on 19th Street?"

"Yes, oh please, yes," I said, rolling my head on the sidewalk in drunken abandon as he lightly dry humped me. If Monika and Ben were cats, Heinz was a friendly puppy dog who always wanted to cuddle and always was humping your leg.

"We'll go to the party, I promise," I said, "but please let's just stay like this for a little while longer. I don't want it to end."

"It's not going to end, silly," Heinz said. "It's just going to *change*, that's all. C'mon, we've been here long enough, let's go to the party." He pulled me up off the sidewalk. There were no people on the street right then.

"Stop looking so open and shy and cute," Heinz said. "You're driving me nuts!" He opened his mouth on my mouth again. We did that standing there in the street, upright. It was the same sort of kiss as our first one, but it was a sadder kiss, a more adult kiss. Heinz broke it for a moment, but he looked at me and went "ummm ..." and dove back in again, which made us laugh. We started walking like that down the block, locked in a kiss but walking, which was just purely silly. I don't think you can be in love with someone, or at least I can't, if you haven't been truly and deeply silly with them. Silliness is sex in a different key. It's another key to the kingdom.

We did have to break our kiss when we got to the door of the apartment house, which was right next door to the Peter McManus bar. They buzzed us in. We climbed the stairs and the apartment was small and had exposed red brick, just like my apartment on 20th Street had had, and the party was filled with cute gay boys in their twenties and early thirties.

There were dancers and actors and writers and poets and publicists, and everybody was fairly drunk but not too much so, and everybody was rampantly, innocently horny. The good thing about being in such a small apartment with a group like this is that everybody has an excuse to brush up against each other and sit on each other's laps. We sat down on a couch by the kitchen counter, and all the boys got their arms and legs and heads and everything else all tangled up together. The conversation was polite, like some disposable gambit that allowed us to touch each other all over and touch some more.

Heinz was next to me and cuddling me, but he got up and bent over and started shaking his ass in the way that strippers do, or girls in rap videos. Twerking? Incredibly unhot, this ass shake thing, I think, but it was very Heinz—he made this incredibly unhot move hot with his "I'm dumb and sexy!" façade look.

We all started spanking him, and everybody got up after him and got spanked by everybody else. There was nothing particularly lascivious about this. It seemed like the most natural thing in the world at the time. This was a playground for young gay adults, and it was recess for as long as we liked.

I was so used to the heavy, blunt importunings of dirty old men in groups that I was totally entranced by the lightness of all this youthful flirtation. A sweet-looking boy with a shaved head sat down next to us on a couch, and I tried to tell him about our Kiss. "Oh wow, kiss him again," the boy said to me, and so I replicated The Kiss with Heinz on this couch for an audience. It's always better to have an audience! Especially an attentive, loving audience, and this boy was loving and attentive. He stroked our faces calmly as we did our thing. We broke it, and Heinz told the boy that I was going to have a huge hickey soon. "I *so* broke his blood vessels," Heinz said.

Then we were standing by the door, and I was grabbing and being grabbed, and everybody had to show their underwear, and I saw Heinz opening his pants and popping the elastic of his underwear (his was green, mine was white). My eyes followed Heinz as he slid over to the TV set, where he maneuvered a dark-haired boy onto a couch and started very uninhibitedly dry humping him, putting the boy's legs on his shoulders and down behind the boy's ears.

Flexibility! Heinz kept dry humping people and even couches and chairs, and at a certain point he pulled the dark-haired boy and two other guys into the bedroom. They locked the door. They were in there for maybe fifteen minutes, doing whatever needed to be done. I wasn't jealous. But I did wish I could have been one of the four inside the bedroom.

Heinz came out of the bedroom looking all smeared and naughty-boy happy. When he saw me he immediately zeroed in on me, to reassure me, I guess. He kissed my forehead and draped an arm around my shoulder and pulled me close to him as we collapsed back down on the couch by the kitchen counter. "Where do you live?" he asked, and I told him. "OK, we'll go to my place, it's on 26th Street, come here." He put his tongue in my left ear this time.

"What do you do for a living?" Heinz asked suddenly, and I laughed because it seemed like an arbitrary question, or like an arbitrary time to ask that question. "I pose for photos, or something, but I'm also, a writer?" I answered, picking up his Valley Girl thing, and Heinz's face flushed with excitement. "Really?" he said with that upward inflection. He was my upward inflection.

"You know what I've *always* wanted to do?" he asked, and this was a question so I said, "What?" His eyes flashed and his tongue came out of that thick mouth. "I've always wanted to have a thing with a writer where I was like their *slave*, like, naked and tied up all day, under their desk, and while they wrote I would for *hours* and hours on end be their Desk Slut." I told him some of my fantasies, and he said, "That's disgusting! You're so depraved! I love it!"

That seemed like a specific enough cue to kiss him again, and we went into one of our open mouth "umm, umm" kisses that didn't want to ever be broken. As we did, I could feel the other guys below us doing somewhat frenzied jobs of work on our lower bodies. Every now and then I would glance down at who was doing what to me and sometimes I would move slightly and adjust Heinz's body with my hands so that they could get easier access to it, and this adjustment was so *deeply* hot to me, because it was like he was my guy, my lover, my sweetheart, my sex toy, and I was magnanimously loaning him out or sharing him with others … as if I were saying, "Oh, you want that part of him, wait, let me make it easier for you. Let me make it so you can have *unfettered* fucking access to him."

Things resolved themselves in a natural way. We slowly got up, still kissing, and the boys pulled up our pants for us and zipped them and everything, and with our pants back on they sort of patted us a little more. It was so warm and friendly. Like they liked us, or like they understood that we were having a serious thing with each other and they were glad to help out or be a part of it.

Hands on your body—it's so easy to tell a friendly touch from a hostile touch, an indifferent touch from a touch filled with good humor, or desire. To be fair, the best of my older guys touched me sometimes in an affectionate way, but their fingers had a melancholy, what's the use? feeling, always. Being with guys my own age, I felt this surge of possibility, and this made the friendly touching much more energizing.

We broke our kiss at the door to say goodbye and grope and get groped some more. That feeling continued in the living room of the awareness that Heinz and I were having a "thing," and everybody seemed so ebullient about it, like they were part of it, or they might find a "thing" themselves, and soon.

Heinz kept his arm around my shoulder as we walked down the stairs and back onto 19th Street. It was 4 AM, or thereabouts, and it was bitter ice cold on 19th Street, but we walked slowly, dreamily. If Monika had been there, she would have said it was very Frank Borzage. In the films of Frank Borzage, the couple is wrapped up in a created world of their own, and the cuddling of a body on top of another body can bring new life into the world, or make old, dying life resurge and reignite and make a pretty blaze to keep warm by.

"Can we stay up?" I asked.

"Of course, silly, we're going to stay up for as long as it takes," Heinz said.

"OK," I said, and I rested my weary head on his shoulder. Nerissa, my little body is a-weary of this great world. "This is it, right?" I said. "Yes," he said, simply. That was a night that I think about all the time.

VII

The Museum of Modern Art was remodeling then, and they were showing
their films in a theater on 23rd Street close to Gramercy Park. The next
day—very late in the afternoon—I took Heinz over there to Gramercy
Park to show him my Perfect Tree Branch. On the east side of Gramercy
Park, there's a tree that has a Perfect Branch. The individual branches on the
large branch are perfectly even, or almost. Calling it a Perfect Branch might
be hyperbole, but it was perfect enough.

"I love it," Heinz said as we stared up at the Perfect Branch on the east
side of Gramercy Park. "I can imagine just staying under it with you for a
really long time in the summer, just walking back and forth under it and
feeling better and better."

"Oh, sweetie," I said, and I kissed him all open-mouthed under the
Perfect Branch.

We went to the box office and I got our tickets. I had actually paid for
a membership a few months back after Ben had sent me a check, so we both
got in free. They were doing a Delphine Seyrig festival, and this was the
day that they were showing Seyrig in Marguerite Duras's *India Song*. We
lingered in the lobby for a moment and leaned against the doors, staring at
each other lovingly. I heard a voice say, "Sontag! Sontag! There should be
tickets under *that* name. Will you check again?"

I looked over at the ticket window and saw a woman standing there
with long thick inky black hair. She was dressed all in black. Of course I
knew who it was. She had said her name. But it took a moment to sink in.
It was almost dream-like.

"Sontag! Sontag!" she cried again, to no one in particular. Imperious,
impatient, but slightly absurd, too, as if she knew she was being over-
dramatic and wanted to give us the pleasure of a diva fit. They gave Susan
Sontag her tickets, finally, and Heinz and I went outside to wait in line.
We stood there for just a few moments before Sontag came outside, too.
She looked sheepish now about her diva fit, and I found this sheepishness
highly attractive, sympathetic. In her slow, sheepish way, she stood behind
us. Heinz looked at me and I looked at him. He knew who she was. I could
count on him.

We waited out there in the cold for fifteen minutes or so, and Sontag kept lightly falling into us and apologizing in a soft, barely-there voice. Almost a girlish voice, but not quite. She was very ill then, I think, with the cancer that would kill her the following year. Ill as she was, she was still willing to wait in the cold with us for a rarely screened Marguerite Duras film.

It got to be a half hour that we were waiting. Still Sontag stood there, uncomplaining, lightly falling into us every now and then, and it felt like some kind of dance. I kept getting little signals from Heinz, like he wanted to say something to her, but I was frozen, too intimidated to talk. I had read Sontag's book of essays *Against Interpretation* over and over again in college and afterward. She was a hero of mine, and the idea of her cheered me up, but I didn't want to seem like some fawning, inane fan. Right before we were let in, Heinz saved me. He turned to her and did his Teeth smile and said, "I just want to say, we *love* your work and we love you."

I looked back at Sontag, and she had a cloudy but also sweetly malicious sort of look on her face. "Thank you," she said. And then, as almost an afterthought, she said to Heinz, "You're very beautiful." Now that is what I call a seal of approval!

Heinz put his head on my shoulder as we filed into the theater. Sontag took her seat up front, in the middle, and she stayed there looking up at the empty screen, unmoving, just like Monika. She was waiting. Heinz and I sat in the back and cuddled a little. We got some sour looks from the MoMa crowd, which made Heinz giggle onto my shoulder.

The film was high-flown and obscure. There was little or no direct dialogue. The words were all narration. The only thing I can remember about that movie now is the way Delphine Seyrig swung her arms to suggest imperialist decay as she walked down stone stairs and walked into rooms, and of course the musical theme, "Cet Amour-Là," or "India Song," which was played over and over again until it was tattooed on my brain. Jeanne Moreau recorded it. I couldn't forget that melody if I tried.

When it was over, Heinz looked at me and opened his mouth and widened his eyes and said, "OK, I love you, and I loved meeting Susan, but please don't make me sit through something like that again."

"I'm sorry!" I said.

"You should be!" he said, and he kissed me. He wouldn't let go, and we stayed like that in our kiss thing until a hand tapped me delicately on the shoulder.

"Well, well, aren't you kicking over the traces!" said Monika. I hadn't seen her in the theater ... where had she been? Come to think of it, Sontag was sitting in Monika's usual spot, and now I didn't see Sontag. Was Monika

Sontag or was Sontag Monika, or what? Sontag Monika! I love the name of one of Sontag's girlfriends, who was an actress, so I'm just going to write it for you to savor: Adriana Asti. It's alliterative, like Sontag's name, and to me it suggests a harsh-tasting Italian liqueur, like Campari, my Campari.

"The traces are all kicked over, it's true. I'm Heinz," said Heinz to Monika, extending his hand like the world's most polite and well-mannered little boy.

"I'm Monika Lilac," she said. "How long have you two known each other?"

"Since last night," said Heinz.

"Since yesterday evening," I said.

Monika's eyes widened. She had really lain on the kohl. "So?" she asked.

"I think this is it," I told her.

"What do you mean, you 'think'!" Heinz said, smacking my right upper arm with both hands. "You don't need to qualify it."

"This is it!" I said, driving my energy to the end of this statement, like actors are trained to do. An upward inflection that isn't really a question.

"Yes, you know almost right away," Monika said. She looked faraway and distant, and I could tell she was enjoying looking faraway and distant.

"Pretty much!" I said. "Though I watched him dance and didn't feel anything one way or another. It was only afterward, when he talked to me in the lobby, that it started."

"Yeah, I was interested in him at first just because he had talked to my boss and seemed friendly with him and that, like, intrigued me, but once we were out on the street, that's when it started for me," Heinz said.

"Ohhh," Monika said. "That's right. Why is the very beginning always so vague like that?"

"I don't know," I said. "I think I saw some of Ben and even heard him talk a little in classes before it happened with him."

"Do you still speak to Ben?" she asked. "Where is he?"

"In Rome, I think," I said.

"Still in Rome. He should come back. I miss him," she said. "Do you think he'll come back?" she asked urgently.

"I don't know," I said.

"Does he talk about me? Has he mentioned me?" she asked.

"The last time I talked to him, um ... he said that he needed ... he needed to feel some simpler, less dramatic things," I said. "He didn't use those exact words." Our actual phone conversation had been blunter and had included Ben using the phrase "uncomplicated pussy," which is what he said he needed.

"It's too much, I'm always too much," Monika said, almost apologetically. "I don't see why. I guess they're afraid. There have been others who weren't afraid, or who weren't afraid for longer periods of time. I would die for him, too, you know. At this point, I would die for him, too. Would you tell him that, when you feel it's right, or if you feel it's right?" she asked.

"Of course," I said. Poor Monika, I felt bad for her now.

"I miss you, too, Robert," she said. "I'll see you soon, here maybe, all right, at the movies?" She clasped my arms with both hands, and I reached out and lightly rubbed her back. When people reach out to you physically like that, you need to touch them back. "Yes," I said. "Soon." And then she drifted away.

"Wow," Heinz said. "Is she, like … OK? Is there something … the matter?"

"No, that's just her," I said.

"She's so beautiful."

"I know. And she has great taste and she gives the best parties. But she's not the world's most stable person."

"I can see that," Heinz said. "We should get up, I guess, but I don't feel like it yet. Do you want to stay for the next movie? It's got to be better than the last one. I liked the actress, what's her name?"

"Delphine Seyrig."

"She's sort of … there and not there."

"Yes."

"She's sort of … an idea of an actress?"

"Yes." If I had any doubts about being in love with him, those doubts were now put to rest for good.

"Let's just stay here and cuddle in the back," Heinz said, "Actually, let's go upstairs and cuddle and maybe sleep a little and we can watch the movie if we want to. Do you have to get tickets?"

"I will if they ask me, but it should be fine. Let's go up to the balcony."

We had the balcony all to ourselves for a while. There was no usher here at this temporary theater. We stared at each other for a long time in the half-light of the theater and traced our faces and what was seeable of our bodies with our fingertips. Our hands moved all over and there was so much to explore, and yes we got hard again, and yes, when two women came up to the front row we just went further up. The movie started, and it was *Daughters of Darkness*, a perverse and elegantly filmed feminist lesbian vampire movie. Heinz and I made love as quietly as possible in the last row as Delphine Seyrig's face filled the enormous screen down below. She was platinum blonde in this movie, and she spoke in English in a buzzy, distracted voice.

Heinz and I committed to pretty much every sexual act we could possibly get away with with our clothes on and without a condom. We kissed and sometimes he pulled my shirt up and licked one of my nipples, and sometimes I briefly pulled his pants down and looked at and licked and squeezed the dirty, private parts of his body as the light from the projector flickered above us and Seyrig murmured this and that and scooped up the ingénue for herself. We fell asleep for a bit, and I woke to another light touch. From Monika, of course. "What a film!" she whispered to me, all excited. "It's the story of my life, that film, don't you think?"

"Yes!" I said, still sleepy but mustering as much genuine enthusiasm as I possibly could. I had seen enough of the film to know that what she said was true, and attractively self-aware. It was one of her rare winning moments when she was not deceiving herself for her audience.

"You know, you're downhearted, and you think, 'What's the use?' and then you see a film like that and it speaks to you and suddenly you're back in business again!" Monika cried in a vivacious, bubbly voice I had never heard her use before. I smiled broadly at her and was happy for her. She was rummaging in her bag and writing something down, and she gave me an almost transparent bit of paper with an address and a phone number in purple ink. "That's where I'm living now, dear, so just come on over with your boy whenever you'd like, OK?"

"OK, Monika, that would be great!" I said, and I got up and hugged her, and then she high-kicked it out of there.

When I sat back down, Heinz rested on my shoulder and let out a contented purr. "Is there another movie?" he asked plaintively. "Can we stay?"

"I think we're going to have to go," I said.

"You mean there isn't another movie?"

"No, but let's go to my place and we can watch something there if you want ... I mean, if you still want to keep seeing me."

"Hey!" he cried, tickling me a little. "Stop that. Of course I want to see you, I want to *see nothing but you*."

"OK," I said, all tearfully grateful.

So we rented *Brief Encounter* from Kim's, and the mean hipster straight male staff looked at me funny, standing there with my hot Lederhosen Slut, and we went back to my place. Heinz gasped when he saw my apartment. "Fuck! Wait! Fuck! Get! Out! This is *crazy*! You *pay* for this place?"

I fumbled and mumbled something about it being cheap.

"OK, Bobby. OK, I'm just going to lay this out, we're young still, we can be reckless. Will you be reckless with me?"

As if he even had to wait for my, "Yes!"

"You're going to move your few pitiful belongings to my place and we're going to shack up, like my grandmother would say. This place doesn't have a lease, right?"

"It's a weekly thing, actually. I can leave whenever I want."

"Well, that's the one thing this place has in its favor. My roommate is away, like indefinitely, so you wouldn't even have to pay rent for a while."

"You'd like the company?"

"Yeah, *Bobby*, I'd like the company," he said teasingly. We kissed, but he shuddered and shook me off. "But let's take our movie and go to my place. I can't stand it here. Oh, wait, fuck!"

"What?" I asked.

"I need to get a new DVD player. We won't be able to watch your movie. Can you keep it or show it to me later?"

"Sure," I said, a little disappointed. "It's just a sad romantic movie I like."

"I love you!" Heinz said. Just to remind me. "I love you, too," I said. I shyly looked down at the floor.

We went back out into the night and Heinz hailed a taxi before I could stop him. "I have some money, I'll pay for it, I'm not extravagant, I know how to save, but I like a taxi sometimes, and right now we need a taxi," Heinz said, all in a rush of explanation as we got in, and away we went.

We shacked up and mostly hid from the world together that winter, only going out to booze it up at the nearby Chelsea gallery openings on Thursday nights. I was still hanging on to my "art world denizen" persona, which I thought would impress Heinz. This was the point when all the galleries had moved to Chelsea, and they were all in these giant industrial buildings between Tenth and Eleventh Avenue between 20th and 29th Street, but mainly concentrated between 23rd to 26th, or at least that's where Heinz and I concentrated. A lot of them were what Heinz called "vanity galleries," places that would show just about anybody. There was so much room in all of these buildings that hundreds of little galleries kept popping up everywhere.

The big ticket galleries for us were Betty Cuningham on 25th Street, where waiters served you fairly good white wine from trays, and Cheim & Read, also on 25th, where they set out plastic cups of white wine and you could just grab as many as you liked. ClampArt on 25th Street was fun because that's where all the hot guys were. Cheim & Read was the rich gay establishment place, and ClampArt was its rambunctious twink little brother. We were also partial to the Caelum Gallery on 26th Street, which featured lots of Japanese art. And fizzy red wine and chocolate donut holes at their openings.

I can't say that I remember much about the art we saw; a lot of it was bad, of course. But I do remember how delightfully tipsy we were after, say, our fifth glass of white wine as we walked up and down staircases and made out in staircase landings and rubbed shoulders with colorfully dressed characters and sometimes paused for a dirty quickie in one of the washrooms in 511 West 25th Street, which had a good mix of vanity galleries and semi-serious galleries.

Afterward we would sneak into our favorite gallery, the wondrous Amsterdam Whitney, which was run by an eccentric couple who were always in some kind of kooky evening dress. The wife was short and blonde and always busting out of her long black gowns, and the husband wore a suit and tie but sported kilts down below. He was forever saying, "We're aristocrats!" to people at the door, sometimes proudly, sometimes defensively. Well, maybe they were.

We went to the galleries to eat as well as drink. At the Amsterdam Whitney, there were piles of good desserts, cakes, cookies, and you were supposed to RSVP, but Heinz talked us in. They had theme openings. "Come as your Mid-Winter Madness," said the invitation by the door, and Heinz and I laughed discreetly at the outlandish costumes we saw as we quickly chewed our free cookies and cakes. There was lots of glitter, lots of skin, lots of white fur.

One girl always went to the gallery openings in the nude. Her entire body would be painted, and a man, probably her boyfriend and probably the guy who had painted her, would shepherd her around and protect her from drunken, wandering hands. Heinz would pull me into various alcoves to make out. Umm, umm, umm. Our kisses got deeper and deeper as we got drunker and drunker.

We did a lot of drinking together. We lived together for a year. He was the miracle I had waited for. He was my age, and he was the sexiest boy on earth. And he wanted to be with *me*. We hid out. We danced. We cooked. We had indelible sex that barely ever ended. I lost all self-consciousness and furtiveness. Heinz thought I was sexy, and so he made me sexy, and that healed a lot of wounds for me.

Then we fought and broke up, mainly over my lack of political engagement. I didn't really want to march with him against the second Iraq war. I tried, but I wasn't a protester, and Heinz was. But really the bigger problem always underneath was that he knew I was still in love with Ben. And he tried to be cool about that but eventually he hated it. He called me "self-loathing" for still wanting Ben so badly, and hanging on his every whim and phone call, and that stung. I guess you could say I was immature, and that I didn't fully appreciate what I had in Heinz.

But I was made that way, or forged in that crucible. There's only so much you can do to change who you have been made to be, at least when it comes to romantic desire. Deep down, I cared most keenly about straight guys and their approval. The worst thing of all to admit is that the most exciting sex with Heinz didn't stand a chance against Ben Morrissey looking at me in a flirtatious or mock-flirtatious way, or sitting close to me, or putting his long legs over mine. But that's the nature of desire. The promise of desire unfulfilled is lodged in you, even when you forget it and think it means nothing anymore. The fulfillment of desire doesn't stand a chance because it isn't so mental. Everybody wanted Heinz. He was a very coveted guy, a prize. My Heinz, he was mine for a year.

Ben met Heinz once. He clapped me on the back afterward and told me that Heinz was "so hot," and he got all macho and said, "Kudos, kudos, my friend." But he looked uneasy. He ran his fingers through his hair. He looked like he wanted to punch somebody. "Your guy is so hot," Ben repeated in his most distracted voice. He seemed jealous of Heinz, but he also seemed fully aware that he had no right to be jealous at all. This was quite a conundrum, but I could see that it amused him, too. Eventually he looked a little sly, and he said Heinz was "so hot" a third time ... but "hairy," which of course he famously didn't like.

Heinz left to go on a tour, and he told me to leave our apartment. He moved on. I still dream about us getting back together. I still talk to my pillow as if it were him. I know, I know. I'm sure you've never done anything like that yourself. I've only seen Heinz a few times after he broke up with me. I would see him very briefly at a party or at an opening. He always acted like he wished he didn't have to see me. He didn't pretend to be friendly. I had disappointed him. I desperately wanted him to be the Heinz from 19th Street again, but he wasn't. That boy is gone. Heinz wanted me for a year. I cling to that when I need to, which is always.

My favorite Heinz memory. We've made love all night. It's 5 AM. I put on a Billie Holiday recording, "Some Other Spring," and grabbed Heinz up in my arms.

"Do you like Billie or Ella better?" I asked.

"Why do I like have to choose?" Heinz asked.

"Because you do," I said.

"Ella," Heinz said, unhesitatingly.

This surprised me. Almost everyone went for Billie when I asked this question. Ben and Tanya and so many other people, they all said Billie. Only one other person had said Ella Fitzgerald without hesitating, and that person was Monika Lilac at Film Forum as we came in out of the winter slush to see something or other. "Ella!" she cried, almost indignantly, and she didn't elaborate, and I wouldn't have asked her to.

"Why Ella?" I asked Heinz.

"Because it's harder to be happy," Heinz said.

VIII

I was alone again, and I started going out to bars. Nothing had changed. In fact, things had gotten worse. What I dreaded was someone saying something disparaging about my looks. What I wanted most was a compliment on my looks. And after a few insults that I couldn't manage to avoid, my self-esteem reached its lowest point. I had started working in a low-level job at a publishing house, and it was pleasant and undemanding but lonely and anonymous.

Then there was a party on Easter in 2004. I had read about it in *HX Magazine*. It became an infamous party, actually. That's where I kicked into a different gear. I became someone else for a bit. It was like acting in a way. If you're iffy, you learn to be an actor, and you learn how to fool people. Heinz had somehow been fooled. Maybe other guys might be if I played my cards right.

It was Easter Sunday night in Manhattan, and I put on my old "Sex Hat," my now-battered black baseball cap, which functioned much like the bowler hat that Sabina wears in Milan Kundera's *The Unbearable Lightness of Being*. For me, as for Sabina, this hat meant that all bets were off: my contact lenses went in, my tight blue jeans were pulled up over my tingling lower body, my shark tooth necklace a girl gave me in high school was pulled down around my thick Irish neck.

I looked in the mirror and said, "He's coming … he's coming … watch out … he's *coming*." Then I pulled The Hat down on my head, and my personality underwent a full-scale, freakish metamorphosis. I was no longer solitary and diffident, as I was during the daytime. A nighttime creature now, I bolted out of my furnished room and lightly jogged down to this party that was being held in a bar on Orchard Street near Delancey.

It was just far enough downtown to seem illicit, as if you could do anything and no one would know or report back to the authorities, whomever they were at the moment. It was a party hosted by Rudy Hardy, a renegade promoter and notorious libertine who staged his events with the care and showmanship of a P.T Barnum or a David O. Selznick.

I entered the dimly lit space at 9 PM on the dot. One cute blond bartender was drowsily setting up, and I happily took a seat on a stool. There was an hour of open bar from 9 to 10 PM. As an open bar professional, I knew the exact amount of free vodka tonics I needed to get just drunk enough for the rest of the evening, roughly one every ten minutes or so, with a rogue seventh drink right before the free booze became overpriced cocktails for suckers.

After my second vodka tonic, the blond bartender shut the black velvet curtains over the front windows and the whole space became ominously darkened. A few men started to drift furtively in. I talked to all of them, my social inhibitions killed by the alcohol. Some of the men were visiting from Europe, and some were performers of one sort or another. There was a contortionist who did some grotesque poses on the floor until I begged him to stop putting his legs behind his head.

I saw Rudy Hardy himself come in, a tall, dark-haired, preoccupied man who shot over behind a console and started to crank up some loud music. I went downstairs. I sipped the last of my vodka tonic, which seemed unusually strong all of a sudden, and a heavy older man who looked like the actor Rip Torn came down and gave me the fish eye. I went back upstairs, and I was very nicely starting to feel the liquor in my legs and in the muscles of my mouth.

The upstairs bar had grown crowded, noisy, and there were stray, over-confident blonde women hungry to see the gay party animals, anxious to rest from their battles with the opposite sex. I drank my sixth vodka and then cadged my fail-safe seventh free drink at 9:54 PM, just to be safe. Around 10:30 or so, I was drunk in the best possible way, and I talked to anyone at hand, fairly coherently.

This was a real downtown party. The singer Justin Bond beamed like a proud mother at the stable of boys who were beginning to float around the bar. I weaved over to the door and fell into a dressed-to-kill Rufus Wainwright. Like long-lost sisters, we talked for a time about obscure female vocalists, from June Christy to Lee Wiley. "I hope I don't die," said Rufus suddenly when we ran out of names from the past.

At a certain point, around 11:30 PM, a pair of black velvet curtains parted at the back of the space. A large wooden cross came into view. Then, on cue, a time-haltingly beautiful young man wearing only a loincloth materialized. He had long brown hair, a sexily fleshy yet perfectly proportioned body, and a mysteriously solemn face, a mask with tiny brown eyes, a long, straight nose, and full, immobile lips. Slowly, this uncanny person took a crucifixion position against the wooden T.

The noise started to die down in the bar. Almost everyone was uncertainly staring at what seemed to be some kind of burlesque act. Two big men who looked like bouncers tied the young man's arms to the cross, and the crowd let out a collective little gasp, for the young man really did look eerily like Jesus, or at least the images of him on holy cards the world over. I inched my way closer to the scene, tentatively. The crowd was hushed now.

At exactly the right moment, the two bouncers kneeled down and roughly yanked the loincloth off this go-go boy Jesus, and he was erect. Go-Go Jesus's face took on a forbearing, weary expression as his head sank back into the cross and a few flashbulbs went off. Parts of the crowd shrieked in what sounded like pain, or pleasure, or surprise.

There was nervous tittering on the outskirts of the crowd, but a rumbling sort of sexual energy was obviously building. Finally, an extremely drunk, heavy-set middle-aged man kneeled down in front of Go-Go Jesus. The man stayed there indefinitely, and this decisive action was greeted by a smattering of applause and a few very nervous titters. I fixedly stared at Go-Go Jesus's face, which remained as stoic as a sphinx in the desert.

A sly-looking, dark-haired pretty boy knelt behind Go-Go Jesus. The crowd started to rustle with excitement and there were some eruptions of Rabelaisian laughter. The crowd became loudly boisterous. After a while, the boys and men in the bar showed no restraint or shyness whatever when it came to Go-Go Jesus. In pairs and groups they applied their mouths and hands and tongues to practically every part of his body, as if it were the Depression and they were starving and here was a free hot lunch.

After about two hours of mauling, Go-Go Jesus was let down from his wooden cross and disappeared downstairs. I went downstairs after him. Way down in the back, an impromptu orgy had commenced. A performer and downtown personage named Dean Johnson, who was six foot six inches tall and bald, was naked in the middle of the action and looking like a lurid Christmas tree.

The Rip Torn ringer who had given me the fish eye earlier in the evening silently approached me and started to feel me up. From behind his turntable, Hardy glanced at me. I quickly unbuttoned my jeans and yanked them and my underwear to the floor. The Rip Torn ringer whispered, "You're beautiful," in my ear. Hardy looked at me briefly and smiled his sharkish smile. I loved him then.

I sent a brazen email asking Hardy if I might go-go dance for him at one of his parties. I attached my two best Ben Morrissey photos, and another more casual shot that was somewhat more explicit. I said that I'd be happy to audition for him.

I got an email right back, friendly, to-the-point, interested. Hardy wanted to see me right away, at his place, to audition. I got his address in Brooklyn and got showered and tarted up and took the subway out to Williamsburg, wearing my increasingly tattered Sex Hat.

I rang the bell, and Hardy answered the door in his underwear. He towered over me. His imposing, tight, fit body was mostly shaved. Dark hair, Italian, I think, maybe part Italian. Hardy seemed distracted, and even a little shy, which surprised me. "Nice, man, so let's see you," he said amiably.

With a confident sort of speed, I walked over to a window and pulled down my pants and underwear and looked over my shoulder at Hardy, who was sprawled on a futon and smiling his shark smile. "Cute," he said.

"I'd love to dance for you," I said. "You wouldn't even have to pay me."

"I'll pay you, that's cool, you can dance for me," Hardy said. I think he was secretly sort of a nice guy.

I read in *HX Magazine* that Hardy was giving a party devoted to absinthe, the cloudy, green alcoholic drink that supposedly rotted the brains of Rimbaud, Verlaine and other lesser Bohemians of the nineteenth century. I sent Hardy an e-mail reminding him of the audition, and I asked if I could dance at the absinthe party.

"Can you be our naked slave barback, too?" came the reply five minutes later.

I wrote back, "Yes."

On the night of the party, I walked west on 14th Street and made my way to the narrow building on 14th and Ninth Avenue where Ed Harris had committed suicide in the film of Michael Cunningham's *The Hours*. In my mind, I think of this freestanding, triangular building as the ne'er-do-well drunk gay cousin of the Flatiron Building.

A rickety elevator took me to the fifth floor, and no one much was there yet, just a few familiar faces who went to every vaguely sexual gay event in New York. A soft-looking, blondish man with a mustache, having availed himself of the clothes-check, walked around stark naked.

I asked the bartenders if I could help, but they said they were fine for now. Hardy entered and went directly to the turntable, cranking up the music. I approached him cautiously. "Bobby Quinn! Sure!" Hardy said. "Just ask the bartenders if they need any help." I asked again, but they said again they were fine.

I had my first absinthe, which tasted like a much stronger version of Pernod, and I sipped it carefully as I watched a bartender set up an absinthe machine that spewed out the liquid from spigots right into glasses topped by spoons holding sugar cubes. I had my second absinthe and journeyed to the back of the triangular-shaped space, where Ninth Avenue traffic seemed to be rushing right at the building. I walked to the center of the space and saw a middle-aged man with pop eyes looking all around him speculatively. I finished a second absinthe, and a third and a fourth.

That was enough. Now I was ready. I took off my sweatshirt jacket and folded it and put it in a dark corner near a platform in the middle of the space, and I took my shirt off and placed it on top of my jacket. I turned and quickly looked at the pop-eyed man, who was staring straight at me, his eyes bright with anticipation. I walked over to the platform and boldly climbed on top of it, feeling the absinthe coursing through my body.

I stretched my arms up, arched my back, and looked over my shoulder at the pop-eyed man. Slowly, I eased down my jeans to reveal the new blue printed pair of Lycra underwear that I'd bought for twelve dollars at H&M earlier in the day. I tossed a wary look at the pop-eyed man, who was unashamedly staring at my body and smiling. I turned forward and sighed drunkenly. This was true happiness!

I climbed down and took my jeans off and placed them in the pile by the platform, and I climbed back up and started gyrating. I was drunk, but not drunk enough that I didn't consciously keep my arms above my head to take attention away from how skinny my forearms are.

A group of older guys gradually started to stand around me, and they were seemingly awestruck. Yes, I thought, I was a miserable and totally solitary high school nerd and now I am an all-powerful go-go boy and sex object! Hardy had given me this platform, and so this platform apparently meant that I was sexy and worthy of worship. That's the way the human mind works.

The men started to approach me with dollar bills. The first dollar bill would be placed shyly, fumblingly, but as the same men kept bringing me more and more dollars, they started to feel that they should have their money's worth. A respectful caress soon became an insistent squeeze and a little pinch and a hard contemptuous pinch and a vengeful spank. Hedonist and pervert that I was, I enjoyed this turnabout into meanness almost as much as I had enjoyed their earlier reverence.

I stared up at the ceiling and I felt hands running up and down my legs, and I looked down at all the dollar bills bulging from my socks. The naked blond man with the mustache yelled, "You're fucking cute!" up at me, and I bent over and gave him a kiss. The naked mustache man put two dollars in my right sock and squeezed my right calve. A creepy-looking older dark-haired guy stared at me steadily and kept saying, "He has a perfect ass" over and over again. This guy didn't tip me, and he kept methodically pulling my underwear down in back when I had pulled it back up. I loved him.

A sumptuous *Playgirl* centerfold model entered the space, fully naked except for shoes and socks, and he began to dance forlornly. His appearance had been advertised in advance. I jumped down from my platform to look at the centerfold's body for a while, and I reached down and got one of my own dollar tips and stuck it in the model's sock. I kept my hands lightly on his perfectly molded, tree trunk legs as the model talked to me and told me about his wife and children. After hearing about school and homework and Lord knows what else, I ambled back to my high platform and started dancing some more.

Men crowded around me as I lowered and pulled up my underwear over and over again. I kept looking at the *Playgirl* centerfold with his beautiful body and practically no audience. This straight model was a hundred times better looking than I was, but I was gay and energetic and drunk and trashy, and he was straight and embarrassed and reserved, and so the party guys ate me right up and left him all alone. Without shame I can say that this turnabout was one of the happiest moments of my life. It was satisfying to me on the deepest level.

Finally I went to the restroom and slowly counted all my money: forty-three dollars in crinkled, rolled-up, moist, hilariously disgusting singles. I placed them back in my socks and went outside to get my clothes. The pop-eyed man was standing right by them. "I was guarding them," he said. I hugged him and kissed him on the lips. The orgy had commenced. It must have been 4 AM.

I put on my clothes and darted over to Rudy Hardy at his turntables. "Hey, Rudy!" I said.

"Bobby Quinn!" Hardy shouted. "You're a real trouper!" He gave me a few twenties and slapped my butt in a friendly but also sexily proprietary way, as if he owned it. I loved that. I staggered home, blissed out, so happy. I danced several more times at his parties that summer and made lots of memories for the old ladies' home.

When I told Ben that I was dancing at these parties, he got very stern and moralistic. He failed to see any humor in it or pleasure. He was the patriarch, and he disapproved. Once I came to Ben from dancing at a particularly debauched Rudy Hardy party and scattered fifty or so crinkled dollar bills on the floor of his hotel room. "These are for you," I told him.

IX

Susan Sontag died on December 28th, 2004. No more screenings, no more string quartets, no more literature, no more theater. Just black out. No wonder she fought so hard for so long. When she first was diagnosed with cancer, Sontag said that she took some solace in a popular song, the Bee Gees' "Stayin' Alive." A rare pop culture admission from a woman who devoted herself so much, in her later life, to high culture, to high seriousness. She had fought off this death in her body for as long as I had been alive.

She had offended nearly everyone when she had written, shortly after September 11th, that we should by all means grieve together, but we should not be stupid together. Hard medicine then. The correct response sometimes is. I'm sure she had her faults and her peccadilloes. Apparently she was mean to waiters in restaurants, according to a recent memoir by a woman who knew her. She could be cruel when she was being dismissive. But she's a Dark Lady of Manhattan culture. And the idea of her is still a living example to me. She was buried in Montparnasse Cemetery, in Paris. "Not bad," bitched Gore Vidal later, "for a graduate of Hollywood High School."

In the mid-aughts I was still working at my publishing job, and time passed slowly for me, emptily. Then Ben had an opening at a Lower East Side gallery in the spring of 2008. I went by myself. I hadn't seen him in a while. I would get letters and emails from Ben, and sometimes a check. I felt outraged, somehow, when he sent me random checks as if I were a charity case. But of course I cashed them. I'm not that proud. We drank together a few times when he was in Manhattan. We had a fight or two. We drifted apart. There would be spaces in our telephone conversations that neither of us knew how to fill.

It was a mild day in 2008, maybe seventy degrees, one of those rare perfect weather days in Manhattan. I was dressed to kill, I suppose, but I still felt out of place, even dowdy, next to the hipsters on the street. I got there ten minutes before 6 PM, when the gallery was scheduled to open, and there was already a sizable crowd outside. Mostly in their twenties, mostly younger than Ben and I were now. We had both crossed Joseph Conrad's shadow line over the age of thirty.

Blanche DuBois in *A Streetcar Named Desire* is only supposed to be thirty, and at thirty she says she's "fading now." Was I fading now, too? Had my moment come, and had my moment passed? In some ways, I suppose so. I couldn't really be a hot young thing anymore, if I ever really had been. When I went inside, I saw all the new naked young people that Ben had photographed. They were in groups and they were naked on landscapes and in caves and near bodies of water. Ben traveled with them and took these photos.

I looked at the cans of Budweiser in the front of the gallery, and I've never wanted a drink as much as I wanted one right then, a cold beer to soothe my wobbly sense of self. But I had stopped drinking. I laugh if someone says I'm in "recovery." I was a drunk, and I stopped drinking, and that's that. There came a night when I fell and I didn't remember falling, and I woke up with three large cuts on my face. It wasn't long after that when I reached for a beer and stopped myself for good. Liquor was going to kill me, and I loved being alive too much.

It was easy to get lost in this crowd. I didn't know anybody, and nobody looked familiar. I talked to a girl who had a tattoo on her wrist that read, "Don't blame me," so I asked, "Don't blame you for what?" She said, "I don't know. It was just supposed to be funny, or something. I was so wasted when I got it that I can't even remember!"

Ben came out in his standard blue agnès b. suit, and he looked exactly the same. He never seemed to change. He was smiling and clapping people on the back, and getting into intimate conversations with all of his models and all the older, moneyed people who kept Ben in business. Just thinking about knowing and talking to all these people made me feel exhausted. But Ben was in his element, giving just enough time to each person, making them feel special, and why not?

Nevertheless, from my over-thirty vantage point, Ben's attention to everyone seemed a little promiscuous, maybe even … slightly insincere? I was in no position to judge him. I have been insincere and dishonest practically on a daily basis for a long time. Well, not on a daily basis, but more than I would like, at work, and sometimes at parties.

It was hot in the gallery, and I was sweating through my formal clothes. I stared at Ben for a while, making his moves, and I tried to look at the photos, but people were always standing right in front of them. Whenever Ben got fairly close to me, I always ducked and went to the other side of the gallery.

At 8 PM or so, it was dark outside. I stood by the door of the gallery to get some air. I watched the crowd disperse, and it dispersed very slowly. They didn't want to leave. After I scurried about a half-block away, I saw

Ben come out, and he was hugging girls and smiling. I saw him talking to Arthur. He put his arm around Arthur's shoulders like they were the oldest of buddies and he couldn't have loved him more.

Maybe I'm naïve. But that shocked me. What shocked me was that this *didn't* seem insincere on his part. But again, maybe I'm over-reacting. Maybe it was all insincere. That's what versatility is? That's what I sometimes admire, after all. All I know is that I felt crushed, anonymous, like some old whore who had hung around Manhattan too long who had been kicked to the curb, and don't bother coming back, you're banned from this bar permanently.

I followed behind them for a bit, a half-block away, and Ben never took his arm off Arthur's shoulder. Arthur's influential wife was there with them, but off to the side, of course. She knew the score, I suppose. Then again, you never can tell with wives like that, even today. She was surprisingly sweet looking, with dark hair and apple cheeks. I sensed she could give Monika Lilac a run for her money when it came to self-deception. Then again, there is a certain type of ultra-complicated woman who only certain gay guys truly have enough time for.

I followed them further and further downtown until Ben and his posse ducked into a once-trendy (still trendy?) restaurant called the Odeon in Tribeca. I stood outside for too long, staring in, looking at the young and pretty and the older and rich dressed-up people inside. I was not young and pretty, and I was not old and rich. And my connection to Ben Morrissey felt tenuous all of a sudden, like a dream, or a barely discernible fuzzy drunken memory. Maybe I didn't know him. Maybe it hadn't really happened.

I started going to repertory screenings again, almost every day, to the Museum of Modern Art and Film Forum, and the Anthology Film Archives, which was as dilapidated as ever. I kept an eye out for Monika, but she seemed to have vanished, from life and from the Internet, and who can tell which is which at this point?

One night the lights came up at a screening of Ernst Lubitsch's silent version of *Lady Windermere's Fan* at the Anthology, and I saw a woman sitting in the seat that had been Monika's, but she was all covered up in what looked like veils of mourning. I thought it might be her, but I thought it can't be. I had to find out before she disappeared. If it was Monika, she would manage to evaporate once she left the theater. I went over and I shyly touched this woman's shoulder. She did not react. "Is that you, Monika?"

Still she did not move. I wondered if there was anyone at all in there. You can dress as eccentrically as you like in Manhattan and particularly in screening rooms, but this woman's get-up was so extreme that it might have been absurd if it hadn't had a touch of the Gothic about it, a touch of the poet. The woman said, "Have you read about what the Nazis did?"

This was too much. I almost laughed, but I didn't. Was it Monika? Was it what was left of her? I couldn't tell. The woman got up, and she left the theater. I started to laugh. What the Nazis did is not funny, of course, but the way she said that … well, I think Lubitsch himself would have laughed. What can you do but laugh? I'd done enough weeping.

I got an Evite invitation from Monika Lilac. She was giving a German Expressionist party at a brownstone in Park Slope, and I got all excited. I dressed up as Cesare, the somnambulist played by Conrad Veidt in *The Cabinet of Dr. Caligari*, and I made my way from Williamsburg to Park Slope, which meant transfers to this and that subway line. I walked to the address on that desolate October night, and all the solid Park Slope trees were rustling in the wind ominously, and I entered a real house of horrors filled with paper-mâché flats that twisted every room into off-kilter diagonal perspectives. They can't have cost much, but they were so expertly made that they were highly convincing. In the front room, *The Cabinet of Dr. Caligari* was playing. I stayed in there and watched for a bit before floating upstairs, where *Waxworks* was playing, and *Variety*.

Monika was dressed as the robot from *Metropolis*! All in gold. It looked like she was in the original costume, or as close to the original costume as you could possibly get, but her face somehow peeked out of it. She kept winking at people, just as the "Bad Maria" does in that movie. She saw me, and her face stayed immobile as she clunked on over and winked at me slowly. I took one of the title cards on the kitchen table and wrote down, "How are you, dear?" and handed it to her.

Monika put the title card down and pantomimed her reaction. She made robot movements and made movements as if the robot was malfunctioning. She got back to the measured robot movements again. So much can be expressed through movement. Movement is inevitable.

I nodded in the slow, sleepwalking way of Conrad Veidt as Cesare. I raised my hand and held up four fingers and made devil horns on my head. I wanted to know if she had found Murnau's *4 Devils*, which had been the quest of her life. I hadn't heard anything about it being found, but she had seemed so close to it the last time I saw her. Monika wrote something down on a title card and handed it to me, and it said, "My whole life has been a wild goose chase."

I shook my head to indicate no. And this seemed to please her. She smiled a *La Gioconda* smile. She grabbed another title card and wrote something down quickly and showed it to me, and it said, "Ben?" I wrote down, "He's lost too." Her face went blank, but she regained her composure and started winking at me again, and winking at her other guests. There weren't too many other guests, actually. I wondered why. My silent doughboys weren't at this party. I looked and looked for them.

I went up to the top floor. There was no movie playing up there. Instead, there was a harshly lit room filled with Nazi atrocity photographs. I took a deep breath, and I wanted to leave the room. I wanted to get out, but I didn't. I forced myself to stay and I forced myself to look at the photos from the liberated concentration camps, some of which I'd seen before, some of which I hadn't. I looked at them until I couldn't look at them anymore. And then I pantomimed goodbye to Monika and left, maybe only an hour after I had arrived.

I was too late to join Ben's Facebook page. He had 5,000 friends before you knew it, and that was the limit. So I had to "Like" his fan page. I suppose that should have been sad. But he posted things himself on his fan page, so ah well. I would "Like" some of his posts, and he would "Like" some of mine, on very rare occasions. Ben Morrissey.

Ben invited all of his Facebook friends to another art opening in 2010. This meant that far more than a thousand people tried to get into his steady gallery on the Lower East Side. I was one of them. I got there very early, and I went inside and looked at the photos as long as I could before the swarms of people made that impossible. They were magnificent. I didn't want to like them, I really didn't. In fact, I was pre-disposed not to like them at this point. But Ben had made a leap forward.

The tenderness to people was still there in the photos of the young and the nude, but there was a real formal rigor now, a distance, a cool appraising eye on the fun of being young, and this extra distance made him, I think, finally, a truly and inarguably major photographer and artist. I was just overwhelmed by these photos. I bought a book of them, and it was expensive ($150), but I wanted to have them. I knew the book would sell out almost immediately. The book would probably be a collector's item one day. I suppose that's what I am, really, a collector.

I did my best to ignore the crass underpinnings of this opening. There was a large bearded man with a camera crew, and he was shining blinding lights on everybody. I heard him saying, "When Morrissey gets chicks naked, it's a win-win, my friends!" The models themselves were made to pose next to their naked portraits by photographers, and they seemed both proud and embarrassed. It was art, right? But they were naked! In front of strangers and press people and all the scavengers of this scene. I suppose you could say I was a scavenger, too. I looked at the models with my predatory eyes, and I appraised them just as Ben's camera had, just as his camera had once appraised me and had seemed to like what it had seen.

When he showed up, the crowd erupted. He was looking a little shaggy and even a little the worse for wear. Older, finally, as I was. A man now, certainly, and a man with obligations, responsibilities, and much else. He wouldn't have time now to walk across Brooklyn Bridge with me and watch the sun come up. And if he had, we wouldn't have had too much to say to each other.

But just being with him, being near him, was a warming thing for me. He had been my friend. He had loved me. He was doing beautiful work, still. He might even be remembered. And I was part of that. That was a good deal for me, let's face it. I didn't have to do all that much for my little piece of immortality in those photos. I just had to be open and let myself get swept along by the wind until the wind put me back down again.

The gallery was far too crowded, and at a certain point we were being hustled out. The fire brigade had been called, and I turned to a girl next to me and asked, "Are we being led to the paddy wagon? What's going on?" She said, "I don't know, but it's so exciting!" The street outside was blanketed in people, all of them staring up at the gallery, wanting to get in, but now even the people who had been inside were being evacuated back out.

This crowd looked expectant. They wanted to see something happen. And it could even be something bad, they just wanted something. Ben was standing on the steps of the gallery, and the fire brigade gave him a bullhorn, and he looked and sounded so tired and harried as he asked the crowd to disperse, in the politest way imaginable. The fire chief was asking who Ben was, and he said, "Huh! So is this kid the next Andy Warhol?"

Well, perish the thought. I stood there and tried to give Ben some good vibes from where I was standing, and he looked down and we made eye contact. He held the bullhorn down for a moment and he just looked at me looking at him.

We were alone together for only a moment. For just a few seconds his face was vulnerable and totally lost, and totally hurt in some way. But then he smiled at me. I really died then. Because it was a PR smile. He made a cheesy thumbs-up gesture, and God help me I made one back. I slipped away back into the crowd and away from the gallery. Finally I was on Houston Street and I could breathe again. You can always breathe on Houston Street. You can call me a Houston Street Queen. The wideness of Houston Street always calms me down.

The next day there was lots of coverage of the opening and pictures of

Ben with his bullhorn, and later in the afternoon I got an email. The black letters, a new email.

webmaster@benmorrissey.com: Hey there, buddy, it's been way, way too long. Thanks so much for coming to my show. I'm sorry I didn't get to say hello to you. You still Miss Rheingold?

Bobbyquinn@hotmail.com: It was good to see you, sweetie pie. No, I'm not really Miss Rheingold anymore ::)

webmaster@benmorrissey.com: Aw. I miss her. I really do.

Bobbyquinn@hotmail.com: I miss her sometimes too.

Webmaster@benmorrissey.com: Are you all right, like financially?

Bobbyquinn@hotmail.com: I'm fine, Ben. Don't worry. I'm happy. I loved the photos in this show. They were your best yet. They're so good. I bought the book.

webmaster@benmorrissey.com: Thanks, man. Seriously, I love you, Bobby. Please don't be a stranger. I'm sorry I haven't been in touch. I've just been so busy, mea culpa. I feel bad. You know I feel bad, right? I'm sorry. I don't know how to say what I need to say to you. I'm in hell here with this. Just ... I don't know. Please don't hate me. We have these parts, and we play them. Why did I get my part and why did you get yours? I don't know why. Just know that it's bad for me, too. Just in a different way.

Bobbyquinn@hotmail.com: I love you, too.

Webmaster@benmorrissey.com: Always, OK?

Bobbyquinn@hotmail.com: OK ::)

OK. Send. Save. Yes, I printed out this email exchange, so that I could always have it, in a folder with all my other Ben Morrissey memorabilia. For Ben's future biographers, or what have you, but mostly for me. And so I put that aside, because I was able to. I had acquired a certain mindset that could put Ben Morrissey aside finally, or put him in his proper place, anyway.

Monika has disappeared, or she has been lost like one of her silent movies. I'm single still, and so is Ben, apparently. I enjoy chatting with guys online on Adam4Adam before meeting up. I do a lot better that way, actually. It is much better than my old way of getting drunk enough so that I could talk to guys at bars. I don't drink anymore or go to bars. I am very good at online flirting, and I have tricked some really good-looking young guys into sleeping with me, once or twice, before they moved on, before they knew better. That's fine. Sometimes I have felt that I care about nothing but sex and the pursuit of sex, yet I also care almost nothing about the sexual act itself.

There were a few Ben Morrissey openings after that one in 2010, but I keep myself vague now about Ben and his career. There was only one more incident with Ben. I pretty recently wrote that I loved one of his new photos on Facebook. It was late at night, and I was feeling sentimental. And I got through to *him*, not his webmaster. "Bobby!!! How are you?" Ben wrote. I responded with a thumbs up emoji. Which to me was the end of the end of the line for us. We used to pen impassioned hand-written letters to each other in the late 1990s.

I don't fall in love with straight guys anymore. I have lost that kind of idiot hope. You give up the idiotic hopes, and you give up the large-scale hopes, and you give up the small-scale hopes, and you do without hope entirely.

I recently met a young straight boy in his twenties, and I was very taken with him. He was small and beautiful and demure, and he had very sad eyes. He inspired some romantic feelings in me. He looked special, but as if his specialness had been disappointed and neglected. I felt I wanted to restore him, or bring him out. But I would never try to do that now. I see this boy from afar sometimes at parties, and I smile a little and hide from him, because I don't want him to see me or know.

I'm distant from my own feelings for this young straight boy, who is so unlike Ben in every way. I suppose you could call that healthy, or progress. But I feel distant about my feelings for gay guys, too. I stand outside of everything. I guess that's called getting older. We get our moment, and the moment has passed. We should be grateful for our moment. Maybe somehow it can come back to us. Maybe it will come back sideways, or inside out.

One afternoon a long time ago when I was still a virgin, I pretended to make love to Ben in my dorm room at college. I got very deeply into it. I entered another place with my mind. It felt like what stepping into the past would feel like now, maybe. It was forbidden, and I was getting away with it. I imagined what Ben would say to me and what I would say to him. This imaginary Ben was really Ben because he said what Ben would have said, I'm sure of that. I suppose you could say it was like a movie. He saw me and he loved me, and this was a benediction.

What we said was more important than what we did, but I had my hand on his neck and my smile up at him was like a grateful teary sunburst. I was radiant! So relieved. I made this happen. Maybe Ben was having sex with some girl at the same time that I did this. He was always having sex with a girl then, and he pretended they were all equally important to him, but they weren't. So he was a fake, but he was a real fake, or at least he was the best actor in this movie.

When I pretended to make love to Ben that afternoon, the rules were broken and my life was different. This went on for hours, and it was so intensely imagined that I feel somehow that it all actually happened. Was this possible? I cannot bring myself to imagine now what this really was, an isolated and odd-looking nineteen-year-old boy talking to the air and jerking off and making use of a pillow rather than a person. But that's what it was. Looked at from the outside and with unsympathetic eyes, it would be pitiful and grotesque, maybe even laughable. So why am I still so certain that something else occurred?

ABOUT THE AUTHOR

Dan Callahan is the author of *Barbara Stanwyck: The Miracle Woman* (2012), *Vanessa: The Life of Vanessa Redgrave* (2014), and *The Art of American Screen Acting: 1912-1960* (2018). He has written for *The Village Voice, Nylon, New York Magazine, Time Out New York, Sight & Sound*, and many other publications. This is his first novel.